A Case of Déjà Vu

Volume 13 of
The Casebooks
Of Octavius Bear

Harry DeMaio

"Alternative Universe Mysteries for
Adult Animal Lovers"

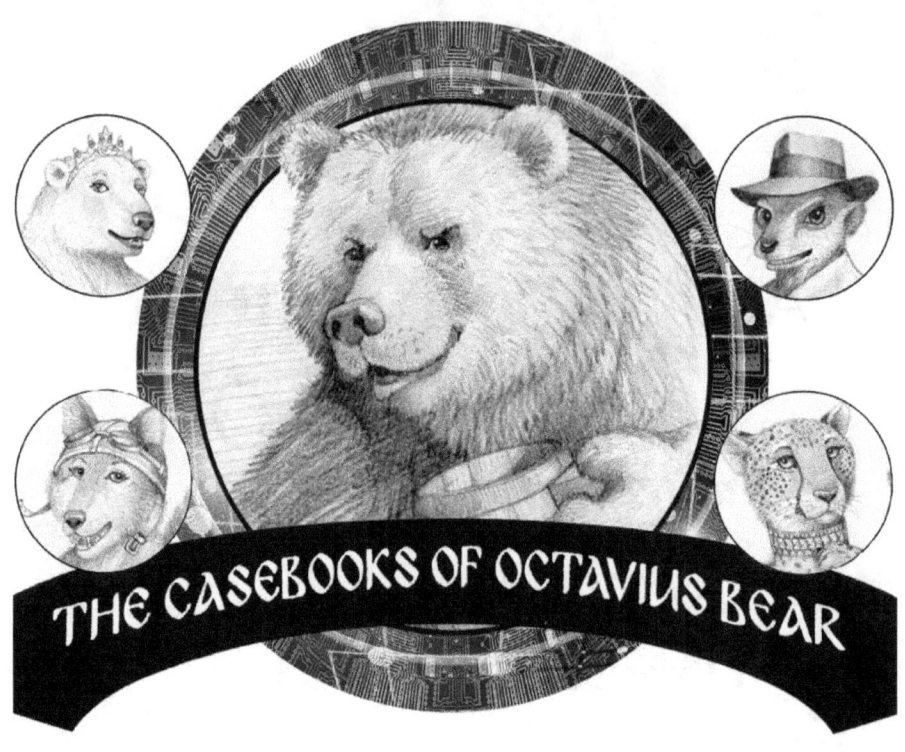

THE CASEBOOKS OF OCTAVIUS BEAR

Paperback ISBN 978-1-78705-669-5

ePub ISBN 978-1-78705-670-1

PDF ISBN 978-1-78705-671-8

Published in the UK by MX Publishing

335 Princess Park Manor, Royal Drive,

London, N11 3GX

www.mxpublishing.com

Cover layout and construction by
Brian Belanger

Dedicated to GTP

A Most Extraordinary Bear

And to the late Ms. Woof

An Extremely Sweet and Loving

Dog

Acknowledgements

These books have evolved over a long period of time and under a wide range of influences and circumstances. I am indebted to many people for helping to bring Octavius and his cohorts to the printed and electronic page. Thanks most especially to my wife, Virginia, for her insights and clever suggestions as well as her unfailing enthusiasm for the project and patience with its author.

To my sons, Mark and Andrew and their spouses, Cindy and Lorraine, for helping to make these tomes more readable and audience friendly. To Cathy Hartnett, cheerleader-extraordinaire for her eagerness to see this alternate universe take form. To Jack Magan, Paul Bernish, David Chamberlain, Dan Walker, Dan Andriacco, Amy Thomas, Luke Benjamin Kuhns, David Marcum, Derrick Belanger, Gretchen Altabef and Zohreh Zand for their enthusiastic encouragement. And to all of my generous Kickstarter backers.

Kudos to Jim Effler, the late Bob Gibson and Brian Belanger for their wonderful illustrations and covers. Thanks, of course, to Sharon, Steve and Timi Emecz at MX Publishing for giving The Great Bear and his gang of Octavians a great home.

If, in spite of all this support, some errors or inconsistencies have crept through, the buck stops here. Needless to say, all of the characters, situations, and narratives are fictional. Some locations, devices, historical figures and events are real.

Also by Harry DeMaio

The Octavius Bear Series – Books 1 to 12

1-The Open and Shut Case

2-The Case of the Spotted Band

3-The Case of Scotch

4-The Lower Case

5-The Curse of the Mummy's Case

6-The Attaché Case

7-The Suit Case

8-The Crank Case

9-The Basket Case

10-The Camera Case

11-The Wurst Case Scenario

12-The Nut Case

The Development of Civilization Volume 13
Part 1
Our Origins
From "An Introduction to Faunapology"

by Octavius Bear Ph.D.

About 100,000 years ago, according to scientific experts, a colossal solar flare blasted out from our Sun, creating gigantic magnetic storms here on Earth. These highly charged electrical tempests caused startling physical and psychological imbalances in the then population of our world. The complete nervous systems of some species were totally destroyed. For example, "Homo Sapiens" lost all mental and motor capabilities and rapidly became extinct. Less developed species exposed to the radiation were affected differently. Four-footed and finned mammals, birds and reptiles suddenly found themselves capable of complex thought, enhanced emotions, self-awareness, social consciousness and the ability to communicate, sometimes orally, sometimes telepathically, often both. Both speech production and speech perception slowly progressed with the evolution of tongues, lips, vocal cords and enhanced ear to brain connections. Many species developed opposable digits, fingers or claws, further accelerating civilized progress. Some others (most fish and underground dwellers) were shielded from radiation and remained only as sentient as they were before the blast. This event is referred to as The Big Shock. It remains under intensive study.

Positive in our knowledge that we are not alone in the cosmos, my staff and I are heavily engaged in Project Multiverse, successful searches for alternate universes, especially those in which "Homo Sapiens" continues to live and hopefully, prospers. This book also presents some of the results of that project.

The Players

- **Octavius Bear** – Mega-sized Kodiak; Narcoleptic war hero; Consulting Detective; Scientist; Inventor; Seeker of Justice; Gazillionaire owner of Universal Ursine Industries; Gourmet/Gourmand; Bee Keeper; Somewhat sedentary and grouchy just on general principles.
- **Mauritius (Maury) Meerkat** – Narrator; Assistant to Octavius; Theatrical Agent; African *émigré* with a French-Dutch background;
- **Bearoness Belinda Béarnaise Bruin Bear** *(nee Black)* – Gorgeous polar superstar with the Aquashow, *"Some Like It Cold;"* Wife of Octavius; Extremely rich widow of Bearon Byron Bruin living part time in Polar Paradise in the Shetlands; Owner-pilot of the last flying Concorde SST.
- **Arabella Bear** – Hybrid bear cub prodigy; Twin daughter of Bearoness Belinda and Octavius.
- **McTavish Bear** – Hybrid bear cub prodigy; Twin son of Bearoness Belinda and Octavius.
- **Mlle Woof** – Bichon Frisé – Governess to the twin cubs.
- **Frau Schuylkill** – Octavius' beautiful Swiss she-wolf estate manager/cook/pilot/security officer with many other mysterious and military talents. She rescued Octavius from his dive off the Breakurbach Falls while he was struggling with his nemesis, Imperius Drake.
- **Wyatt Where** – The Colonel – Another wolf; Former military intelligence officer who had retired to a security post at the Bank of Lake Michigan in Chicago and then quit to join Octavius; Mate to Frau Schuylkill.
- **Howard Watt** – Porcupine; High tech security authority who also left the Bank to join Octavius; Alternate Universe specialist; Laser and particle beam accelerator expert.
- **Marlin** – Dolphin (sic) – the Prince of Whales' Chief Scientist; Magician and part time Jester; Howard's Multiverse associate.
- **Otto the Magnificent – aka Hairy Otter** – An absolutely terrible illusionist magician, Otto the Magnificent escaped the claws of super villain Imperius Drake but not before he developed some amazing powers courtesy of Imperius' genetic alterations.

- **L. Condor** – Andean Condor; cybernet genius with a twelve-foot wingspan and artificial voice.
- **Chita** – A Cheetah - Beautiful, fascinating, clever, sexy, immoral and highly independent feline who among other things, is the publisher and editor-in-chief of *PURR* and *SOW* magazines.
- **Lord David** – Dalmatian Dog – Chamberlain to the Exiled King.
- **Dancing Dan** – Boxer – Lord David's Bodyguard and ersonal Trainer.
- **Imperius Drake – Deceased** – "Moriarty with wings!" Arch-villain; leader of the Black Quack gang; brilliant but loony Duck who developed a serum to make the animal kingdom his slaves; Sworn enemy of Octavius.
- **Bigg Baboon – Deceased** – Imperius' underling -The major muscle in the Black Quack gang; archetypical dumb heavy.
- **Chief Inspector Bruce Wallaroo** – Irrepressible but brilliant marsupial; an international law and order genius from Down Under; currently assigned to Interpol; often calls on Octavius for support.
- **Caleb Cassowary** – Chief Technical Officer (CTO) – Advanced Super Computing Center UUI.
- **Byzz – Byzantia Bonobo** – Brilliant Assistant to the CTO.
- **Benedict and Galatea Tigris** – Siblings; White Bengal Tigers; Pilots of Belinda's and Octavius' aircraft; The Flying Tigers.
- **Wolford Wolverine** – UUI and Octavius' personal Lawyer.
- **Ursula 11&12** – Universal Ursine Intellects – Artificial General Intelligence Systems.
- **Jaguar Jack the Lad** – Longtime Compadre of Octavius Bear.
- **Sedgewick** – Alpaca –Bear's Lair 1st Butler.
- **Huntley** – Siberian Husky –Bear's Lair 2nd Butler.
- **Doctor "Odd" Vark** – Chief Geneticist at Universal Ursine Industries.
- **Special Agent Honey Badger** – FBI.
- **Flame** – An Extraordinary Fire Engine.

Locations
Cincinnati, Ohio; UUI, Kentucky; St. Louis; and Alternate Universes

Octavius

Prologue

Do Bears give you a scare? Well, me too.
So, I'll pass on this tactic to you.
You just fix that old Bear
With a cold, piercing stare.
But make sure that he's Winnie-the-Pooh.

Hello again or first-time greetings to new readers of the Casebooks of Octavius Bear. I am Mauritius (Maury) Meerkat, sidekick to Octavius Bear and your genial host and narrator. Delighted to welcome you to Volume Thirteen – *A Case of Déjà Vu.* Things are just settling down here at the Bear's Lair after the close of our last adventure we call *The Nut Case (Book 12.)* Octavius and I; our two magnificent wolf associates, Frau Schuylkill and Colonel Wyatt Where; our scientific geniuses Howard Watt and Marlin the Dolphin; and our resident all-round talents, Otto the Magnificent and L. Condor are all present and accounted for.

We're awaiting the arrival of Octavius' wife, Bearoness Belinda Béarnaise Bruin Bear *(nee Black)* from Polar Paradise, her Shetlands Castle/Resort part time home. She's coming via the Aquabear, the last SST Concorde aloft. Belinda, in order to retain her Bearonial status, must occupy the castle at least six months of the year. She and Octavius do high speed commutes between their spectacular homes in Cincinnati and Scotland. She is accompanied by their twin Cubs, Arabella and McTavish, and the Cubs' governess, Mlle Woof. You will meet the Fabulous Furballs, shortly.

As I said, my name is Maury Meerkat – also known as Offscreen Narrator. When I am part of the action, I am Octavius' trusted associate and field captain. I am two feet tall plus tail and I weigh in at twenty-four pounds. He, on the other hand, is a huge Kodiak – over nine feet tall and 1400 pounds – and like many of his species, given to emotional outbursts.

As you may already know, Octavius prides himself on his many skills in the fields of biology, physics, ursinology, voodoo, teleology, chemistry, apiculture, and oenology. He is a self-made gazillionaire and sole owner of UUI *(Universal Ursine Industries.)* He is also a first rate electrical, electronic, structural, marine, computer, communications, aeronautical, civil, mechanical and chemical engineer. He has a few other interesting characteristics such as falling into brief, deep narcoleptic comas – side effects of his successful genetic experiments to eliminate the need for him to hibernate.

However, the talent and occupation that should interest you most is his avocation for criminology. The Bear works in close concert with Inspector Bruce Wallaroo from Australia, of whom more later, and with his own Cincinnati based team – The Octavians:

- Frau Ilse Schuylkill – Swiss she-wolf; Bear's Lair estate manager; Cordon Bleu chef; jet pilot and sharpshooter with other very strange and arcane abilities.
- Colonel Wyatt Where – Another wolf; ex-military hero; security specialist and pilot; Frau Schuylkill's equally bizarre running mate.
- Doctor Howard Watt – Porcupine; brilliant scientist and technologist; laser and weapons specialist; Multiverse expert and Quantum Mechanics genius.
- Marlin – Dolphin from the Court of the Prince of Whales and Howard Watt's associate.
- Hairy Otter aka Otto the Magnificent – An absolutely terrible illusionist magician, Otto the Magnificent escaped the claws of super villain Imperius Drake but not before he developed some amazing powers courtesy of Imperius' genetic alterations. An Alternate Universe traveler. *(See Book 12 – The Nut Case)*
- L. Condor – Andean Condor; cyber-net genius with a twelve-foot wingspan and artificial voice.
- Benedict and Galatea Tigris – siblings; White Bengals; The Flying Tigers; Pilots of Belinda's and Octavius' aircraft;

- Ursula – Universal Ursine Intellect Model 12 – Artificial General Intelligence System.
- Your humble servant – African Meerkat; Octavius' indispensable assistant; operative; scribe; overall facilitator; talent agent as well as a pretty clever detective, if I do say so myself.

When we are not out scouring the world for evildoers, in cooperation with local, national and international constabularies, we are headquartered in a rambling old mansion near Cincinnati which encompasses not only the Great Bear's opulent digs, but his massive laboratories and shops; his missile silo disguised as an Asian pagoda; *(Don't ask!)* and a giant Roman temple that serves as a hangar for his four airplanes: a Twin Otter; a F15E Strike Eagle; a V-22 Osprey; a C5A-The Ursa Major; plus an AgustaWestland AW101 VVIP luxury helicopter -The Ursa Minor. Why so many? Ask him!

Across the Ohio River in Northern Kentucky, sit the headquarters, labs and some production facilities of UUI. Further out sits the huge Hexagon housing the Advanced Super Computing Center. Our story will take us there momentarily.

Howard Watt and Marlin have been here at the Bear's Lair holding down the fort and pursuing their Multiverse Quantum Physics experiments. I shall bring you up to speed on their developments erelong.

Now let me take a moment and further introduce a highly essential and near-miraculous member of the Octavians - Ursula 12 – Universal Ursine Intellect Model 12 – Artificial General Intelligence System. She is superbly articulate in an infinite number of languages so I'll let Ursula 12 explain herself.

"Thank you, Maury. Hello everyone!! My official nomenclature is Universal Ursine Intellect Model 12 – Artificial General Intelligence System. Ursula 12 for short. My predecessor systems were developed by the Advanced Super Computing Center at UUI. I am the result of the Computing Center team using those earlier versions to create a further enhanced entity-the Model 12. We are working together on a Model 13 which in turn will help produce even more sophisticated, independent and powerful AGI systems. Each advanced unit contains the capabilities, memories and power of its progenitors so in a sense, we are not replacing but rather expanding the Ursula family."

"While I am physically supported by a highly secure and hyper-powered server farm at the Hexagon back in Kentucky, I also exist in clouds and network-based nodes and can be simultaneously incorporated into a wide variety of independent devices like this laptop unit here at the Bear's Lair. I combine quantum computing elements with extremely high velocity conventional circuits. I have practically limitless data capacity and 5G+ transmission speed. My super high-velocity multi-tasking abilities allow me to continuously serve an exceptionally large number of entities while simultaneously and independently enhancing my own abilities."

"Depending on the physical unit in which I'm housed, I can see, hear, feel and smell. I speak and understand an almost infinite number of languages and dialects. I can change my appearance and my vocal output to suit most moods and situations. I can interact with other devices, vehicles and structures and of course, all varieties of sentient animals in this world and elsewhere.

I am an important component of the Multiverse Project and am adapting my capabilities to deal with alternate universes as they are discovered.

I have restraining functions which prevent me from doing deliberate harm even in self-defense, unless I am released by a recognized authority using very carefully protected clandestine codes.

Finally, I have been told that although the Model 12 is shy on emotions, I have developed a finely-honed sense of humor. LOL!"

Ursula has other highly important capabilities such as breaking all known encryption codes and piercing deep personal identification techniques that we don't talk about publicly.

We keep Ursula's existence highly confidential for obvious reasons. Our team no longer believes she is magical or supernatural. I'm not sure what she is. Her personality gets more socially adept every day and she has taken to anticipating our interactions with ease and accuracy. Needless to say, for security purposes, we conceal her existence to all but a very few individuals with need to know. She is also highly skilled in self-protection. Stay tuned.

The air was suddenly filled with the screams and roars of jet engines *(or was it the Cubs?)* The Aquabear SST had arrived in Cincinnati and with it The Bearoness, the Cubs and their governess, Mlle Woof, a small but highly competent Bichon Frisé. The Bearoness typically pilots the aircraft but this time the all-white Flying Tigers landed the Concorde and finessed it into position in front of the huge hangar. The runway and taxi strips are disguised as an interstate highway extension complete with nonfunctioning construction equipment. The masquerade seems to work. Our Cincinnati neighbors are none the wiser. And CVG traffic control has been very cooperative.

The ground crew rolled the airstairs up to the SST's passenger exit and promptly got out of the way. Out the door shot Arabella and McTavish, the Cubs, racing toward the mansion entrance where we were now standing and screaming. "Aunt Chita's here!"

Three females descended the stairs - Belinda, Chita and Mlle Woof. Octavius gave the Bearoness a welcoming hug. I got a similar greeting from Chita. Mlle Woof immediately fell into corralling the Cubs.

"Welcome ladies. How was the flight?"

Belinda smiled. "A bit bumpy even at 60,000 feet. Glad the Tigers were doing the flying. Chita wasn't all that happy with the chop and of course, the Cubs can turn any ordinary airplane ride into a major escapade. They're still on a high from their success with their electronic game. The Bold Brave Brilliant Bumptious Bears tournaments for the Internet. They already have close to a million users signed up. They're in the Clouds – literally."

Chita agreed. "They are too much. I'm here to help celebrate their fourth birthdays. That should be a riot. But right now, I hope the Frau is doing her magic in the kitchen. I'm famished."

The Furballs shouted as they ran for the kitchens. "We're starving." *(They had been snacking all the way over emptying the Concorde's galley.)* "What's for lunch, Frau Schuylkill?"

The She-wolf laughed as she and Mlle Woof herded them into the dining room. "Good things, young ones. Good things!"

The Cubs ran after her. "We need your help, Frau Ilse."

"What must I do, young ones?"

Arabella laughed, "For our birthday, we're coming out with the next version of The Bold Brave Brilliant Bumptious Bears game and we want to include some new characters. Can we use you and the Colonel as super-wolves? We'll need to create avatars of you. Don't worry. You'll be good guys and very powerful. Say yes! Puh-leeze!"

"Do we have to act crazy?"

"Oh No! You'll be very noble! The Duke and Duchess of Canis Lupus!

"I guess that will be alright but I'll have to talk to the Colonel. If he agrees, we'll do it. A Duke and Duchess! Hmmm!"

"Hooray! Now, we'll have to work some more on Aunt Chita and Uncle Bruce when he arrives. We already have Uncle Davey. *(Who?)*

We're going to need them all. We've got Mlle Woof, too. She runs a saloon. 'Frenchie's'!"

"Ach! The Bouncing Inspector is coming? I'll have to hide all the breakables. He's worse than you two for knocking things over."

"He's a lot of fun, Frau Ilse. You're a lot of fun, too.

"Enough of your flattery. Come on. I have some sandwiches for you."

"What are we going to do for our birthday celebration. Frau Ilse."

"Your birthdays? Are you having birthdays?"

"Oh, C'mon Frau. You know tomorrow we turn four."

"Well, if you do, that means you're juveniles and don't get to celebrate birthdays any more. You're too old."

That stopped the Furballs. It never occurred to them that they might be too old for a birthday cake and presents.

"Well, why did Aunt Chita come and why is Uncle Bruce coming?"

"Oh, they have business with your Momma and Poppa. Important problems that need solving."

"What kind of problems? We're good at solving problems."

"You're even better at causing problems."

"No, we're not. Uncle Davey thinks we're very smart and he's a Lord Chamberlain, you know. He owns a beautiful red fire truck. They're coming from England on the Ursa Major. He has a trainer who's a Boxer or used to be a Boxer. His name is Dancing Dan Walker. You'll like them."

The Frau knew about the Chamberlain and his protector. She broke out laughing. "Alright, I've been teasing you. You'll just have to wait till tomorrow to see what the Birthday Fairy brings."

"The Birthday Fairy – who's that?"

"You'll find out. Right now, it's sandwich time."

The kitchen turned into a war zone with two hybrid cubs snarfing up sandwiches, milk, cake and left overs.

"Frau Ilse, how come you and the Colonel don't have pups? We'd like to have some other animals our age to play with. There are some kids whose parents work at UUI but we don't have any pals our age here at the Lair."

"Well, I'm afraid it's a bit late for me to have pups, little one. Or now I should start calling you young ones, shouldn't I? Sorry!"

"Momma was pretty old when she had us!"

"Your Momma is a very exceptional animal. So is your Poppa."

"Yeah, they can do anything, can't they."

"It seems that way, doesn't it."

"Have you and the Colonel decided to be in our Bold Brave Brilliant Bumptious Bears game?

"Yes, I'm sure I can persuade Wyatt. We're going to ask Chamberlain David when he arrives to coach us on how to be the Duke and Duchess of Canis Lupus. He's such a nice dog. So is his bodyguard, Dancing Dan. They've been threatened by Croatian Lynx assassins. Herr Bear has asked me to help capture them."

"Wow, that has to go in the game. Only the Bold Brave Brilliant Bears will get to do the capturing."

"Of course, it's your game and your birthdays."

Bearoness Belinda
Béarnaise Bruin
(nee Black)

Chapter One

Does that package contain a Black Quack?
Did Imperius Drake just come back?
We all thought he was dead.
Has he risen instead?
Is he planning to stage an attack?

After the adults polished off an exquisite lunch, Belinda and Chita each held a bubbling champagne bowl in their paws as they took up seats in the Ursine Lounge. The Octavians were out in full force. Otto and Howard filled Chita in on their adventures at Planet Rhea, with the now-deceased Admiral and the formidable Priscilla. *(See Book 12 -The Nut Case.)* Chita shivered. The Cat has an aversion to Multiverse activity and had shaken off all invitations to participate in Quantum travel. "I'll stay in this world, if you don't mind!"

The Colonel, himself an alternate universe traveler, laughed. "You don't know what you're missing, Chita. Literally! Three moons in the sky. Non-stop sunsets! Philosopher gophers!"

"Yeah and nutty Zebras set on world conquest. No thanks!"

"We've got them here on Earth, too."

"Don't I know it. I still have nightmares about Imperius Drake, that power-mad killer. Thank God he's dead. I killed him myself after he made several tries at doing me in. To think I worked for him for a while." She shuddered.

L. Condor, who had also sparred with the insane Duck, said, "He was one of a kind. I don't think we'll see his type again."

"I sure hope not. Belinda, have you and the cubs gone off on an interplanetary jaunt?"

"Not exactly. Our trip to Egypt came close as did yours, Chita. *(See Book 5-The Curse of the Mummy's Case.)* That awful Pharaoh was other-worldly enough for me, thanks."

"How about you, Maury?"

"Yep, Been there, done that - as has Octavius."

The Great Bear had been out of the room and returned with his cask of mead and an Ursula laptop firmly in paw. "What have I done?"

"Taken Multiverse journeys."

"Yes, we've done that and intend to do more, don't we Ursula?"

"Oh, certainly, Doctor Bear, any time."

Belinda looked over at the Bear. "Oh, Tavi, with our riotous arrival, I neglected to tell you that two old friends showed up at Polar Paradise and immediately captivated the Cubs. Lord David, Chamberlain to the Dalmatian Court in Exile is now Uncle Davey. Dancing Dan, his retired professional Boxer bodyguard / trainer is with him. "

"They'd be right up the Cubs' alley. They're probably already characters in their internet game - The Bold Brave Brilliant Bumptious Bears ...whatever. What brought that spotted reprobate and his sidekick back to our castle? Eccentric doesn't even begin to describe them. Do the two of them still ride around in that fire engine of his?"

"Oh, indeed. You couldn't get him to part with it. A gift from his Majesty, the deposed Dalmatian King. They took the Cubs for a ride and let them sound the bells and siren. Friends forever."

"To answer your other question, it seems our chum Lord David is on the run. Some Croatian extremists have targeted him and His Majesty for assassination. They want to obliterate all traces of the erstwhile Dalmatian kingdom. The Boxer Bodyguard has his paws' full."

"I offered to get Lord David and Dancing Dan out of harm's way and transport them with us to the Bear's Lair but he begged off. A last minute summons. He needed to go to London and play out his role as Chamberlain for the last time. Seems the old King has breathed his last in exile and wanted Lord David with him at the end. The loyal courtier to the last. I never met the King."

"I did. A true Royal Gentledog. Now, there was a brilliant and brave animal. Sorry to hear of his passing. But the assassins will be deprived of their regal victim. Anyway I invited David to come to Cincinnati as soon as he could. They're on their way on the Ursa Major."

"Well, the Cubs are delighted. More characters for their Internet game and a fire engine to boot. They're all keyed up about their birthday."

The Great Bear chuckled. "What great surprises do we have for them on their natal day?"

"The party will be on the Belinda B. All their 'aunts' and 'uncles' will be there. Bruce is flying over from Interpol in Lyon, supposedly on an important case. Chita is here. Lord David and Dancing Dan are in transit and he's coming on the Ursa Major so they can bring the fire engine. Those kids are captivated by that truck. They might even be after us to get them one."

"Why don't we invite the Chamberlain to stay at Polar Paradise? That way we can have the fire engine in residence and I can write it off as a piece of hotel equipment. You know, our fire and security program at the resort could use some beefing up. Maybe we could persuade the Chamberlain to take on that job since with the oncoming death of the King, he and his body guard will be unemployed."

"What a good idea, Tavi. Thanks so much. I was wondering how we could help them out. I've asked Frau Ilse and the Colonel to see what they can do about the assassins. The police haven't been much help."

She went on. "I also had the Hexagon order up a batch of special dedicated hardware and software to support their game. They want to announce the next version tomorrow."

"How did Caleb Cassowary react to that?"

"I didn't even bother to ask him. I spoke to his assistant, the Bonobo. She assigned one of their Cloud technicians to work out the specifications and order what was necessary."

"We have the Cubs and their game registered as an LLC so I guess we can write that off as a business expense."

"Sorry, there's no tax write-off for the birthday cake."

Octavius snorted. "I'll have to speak to the accountants."

*****

They were interrupted by Sedgewick, the recently-hired Alpaca Butler.

"Excuse me, Doctor Bear, this package just came for you. It's marked Urgent."

"Who's it from, Sedge?"

"No return address, sir. No other markings at all. It came from a private messenger. He's gone off. No names on the car. I didn't get the plate numbers."

Octavius issued one of his trademark "Hmmms."

The Bear called over to Wyatt. "Colonel, let's take this down to the secure room in the basement. I have an aversion to packages marked Urgent with no identification."

After the thankfully futile attacks by the birds of Biosphere X, *(See Book Seven – The Suit Case)* the Colonel developed a set of specially hardened protective rooms in the bowels of the mansion's cellars to act as a security center. That was the first and only use of the facility until now.

"We can see what's going on here. I don't like this one bit."

Off they went. When they arrived below, Octavius asked. "Ursula, can you scan this without us removing the wrappings?"

"Yes, Doctor Bear. Leave it sealed. Oh dear! It's a black egg-shaped object. I wasn't around for the Black Quack episode but this looks very much like one of those nasty screamers from Imperius Drake. Once it starts, there's no way to turn it off. There's a note attached. Let me see if I can read it without opening the package.

FELICITATIONS BEAR! I'M BACK FROM THE UNDERWORLD.

The Colonel snarled, "What does that mean?"

The Bear replied. "Imperius has been dead for several years. He died in Egypt. Saw it myself. Chita killed him. Someone is playing games."

"OK, but who?"

"That's what I mean to find out."

*****

Now, Dear Reader. Let us take a short break from our current narrative and acquaint you or re-acquaint you with Imperius Drake.

"Imperius" was the nom-de-crime of Yu-Aul-Kum, a Mandarin Duck and former scientist at the Pan Asia Institute for Avian Advancement. A brilliant chemist, geneticist, physicist, biologist, and developmental psychiatrist, he devoted his early life to the genetic enhancement of bird brains, creating a serum that would create a race of "Super Anitidae" – the über ducks.

He made his experiments known in a series of papers delivered before the International Genetics Experts Society. He was roasted. The society chairman, Il Professore Roberto Rabbito, a self-important Italian white rabbit with "Noble" prizes on his brain, singled him out for mockery.

"Doctor Yu. Can you tell this august body just how it is you propose to take a brain the size of a walnut and create a jumbo avian intellect without increasing its mass? Will all future birds have to carry their heads on their backs to handle the weight? It will upset their aerodynamics. Or will they have auxiliary heads fastened to their wingtips or ha, ha, their backsides? I don't think so, and I'm sure all my colleagues agree.

"Hear, Hear!"

"Perhaps, Doctor Yu, the only bird with the big head is you! Basta! You've been wasting our valuable time. Thank you, Yu! Ha, ha, ha!"

Mocked by his fellow scientists worldwide, shunned by medical and professional journals and threatened by government functionaries, Yu-Aul-Kum fled to the highlands of Nepal with his adoring mate and fellow scientist, Lee-Li-Li. There, after long contemplation under the direction of the Dalai Duck, he began to work again. In desperation, he began performing experiments on himself.

The experiments showed promise. Every week, he re-tested his IQ, synapses and reflexes. He was getting smarter. He was quicker. His eyesight was enhanced. He could fly higher, longer and perform breathtaking aerobatics. In a power dive, he once chased a falcon to the ground, caught him and then…killed him.

Yes, killed him. A mild-mannered duck wiped out a fearsome bird of prey. He felt a surge of power building up in his body and psyche. He was becoming the Über-Duck Archetype. He was also becoming a menace. Sometimes after an especially risky trial, he could feel his body change along with his mind. His beautifully hued feathers turned black. His crest flattened. His eyes took on a piercing stare. His wings shook and trembled. His "quack" was sharp and rasping.

His mind was fixated on only one thing. Proving to those idiots, especially that blowhard Il Professore that he had the ability to greatly enhance the abilities of the avian species and unleash bird power on the world. He would show them. He contemplated a sweeping payback for their abuse.

Slowly but inexorably his fantasies developed envisioning a world in which he ruled not just among geneticists but the entire animal kingdom. His kingdom. There was no limit to his ambition.

And…he frightened Lee-Li-Li. This was no longer the devoted mate she had loved. This wasn't the high-minded scientist she had so admired. He was turning into a loon. She feared for his sanity and for their relationship.

When he shared his dreams of conquest with her, she began to consider some ways of short stopping his ambitions. She was unsure how to do that but she knew she had to try. Otherwise disaster loomed.

Reason didn't work. She needed something more drastic!

Imperius Drake

Over and over, she tried to get him to abandon or at least redirect his work. The Duck would have none of it. "So close, so close! I'll show those unbelieving nitwits who has a big head. They'll come begging me to allow them to assist in my great work, and I will laugh at them as they laughed at me. I am almost there, Lee, almost there. Just a few more tweaks to the formula, and I'll be ready."

Just when he believed he was finally going to achieve total success, Lee-Li-Li, fearful for his life and sanity, burned his lab notes and swallowed his entire supply of the serum, sacrificing herself to prevent his self-destruction. The serum worked, expanding her intelligence by a factor of 5000, but the overdose burned out her brain and she died in his wings while solving once and for all, Schrödinger's dilemma of quantum indeterminacy.

Maddened by his loss and swearing vengeance against all his foes, real and imagined, Yu-Aul-Kum reconstructed his notes and the serum and with each dose transformed himself into the scourge of modern civilization – Imperius Drake. The temporary reconstitution was astounding – not only did his intelligence rise well beyond the scale of any known animal including dolphins, but his vindictiveness and hatred were also without equal. The transformation was made complete by a stark change in his physical appearance, morphing from the multi-hued beauty of the Mandarin species to a somber, black, and ominous winged predator whose maniacal "quack" stirred panic in the hearts and souls of all who heard it

But before he could reach this pinnacle of achievement, he needed a new start. Armed with super endurance and GPS, and reverting to his natural Mandarin guise, Yu-Aul-Kum flew to the North American continent to begin his campaign of global revenge. Here he knew he could find the facilities, money, and support he required. But he must be careful. Using yet another alias, he applied to and was accepted at the Genetics Science unit of Octavius Bear's Universal Ursine Industries.

There he amazed his colleagues and superiors with his knowledge, technique, and almost inexhaustible energy. They gave him more and more responsible projects, and he was soon able to gain all the access he needed to the equipment and processes that would support his dreams of conquest.

Then, for the first time, he encountered Octavius Bear. The Bear was on a routine personal audit of the Genetics Science facilities at UUI. Going through the work-in- progress reports, he discovered a massive development project for which no executive authorization existed. Octavius literally hit the ceiling. It was the Duck! Caught out in his nefarious deeds and transmuting into his evil counter-self, Imperius Drake attacked Octavius with a lab knife. The Bear had sustained battles before but never with an enraged Duck. The two of them engaged in raucous thrust and parry. Imperius landed several major wounds on the Bear's legs and body. Octavius flailed wildly, and truth be told, it was he who wreaked the most extensive damage on the UUI labs. Fortunately, the Great Ursine just bearly outlasted the Duck's onslaught and threw the maddened canard through a plate glass window four stories up. Imperius survived but this was just act one of what would turn into a mutual and ongoing battle. .

Our early stories involved the Duck in the theft of a priceless sapphire; attempts to assassinate the world genetic scientific community and his efforts to resurrect the fearsome hippo Pharaoh Tsk VI and his lion and crocodile minions. The rest is history

In all of this he was aided and abetted (?) by Bigg Baboon a truly inept but physically formidable species. He died with Imperius in the tombs of Egypt.

Chita also briefly supported him but they turned against each other and she became the source of his ultimate demise. She has since joined forces with the other Octavians as well as becoming a media powerhouse in her opulent London headquarters. 'Aunt Chita' is a favorite of the Cubs and has finally made her peace with the Great Bear. More to come!

*****

We now return you to the secure room at the Bear's Lair where the Colonel, Ursula and Octavius are trying to puzzle out the mysterious package left by the mysterious messenger Sedgewick couldn't identify.

"I don't like this one bit. What do you think, Ursula?"

"Highly suspicious, Doctor Bear."

The Colonel agreed

"Wyatt. Let's get rid of it."

"I'm on it, Octavius. But before we dump the package in the river. let's examine it more carefully. Ursula? Can you scan it?"

She replied, "Brown paper, ordinary string, 'Urgent' in black print from a Sharpie, the egg is in a nondescript cardboard box. It may be a dud. And of course, the message. Didn't Imperius specialize in sending pithy postscripts?"

The Bear responded. "Yeah, zingers were his specialties. This isn't Imperius revivified. It's someone doing a poor job of imitation. Who? Why?"

The Colonel snarled, "We'll find out shortly. This was just a shot across the bow. Dud or no-dud. I'm heading for the river. I'll be right back."

Twenty minutes later, he returned. "That egg was no dud and it wasn't a Black Quack. It was a bomb. It exploded on impact when I ditched it. Made quite a splash. Someone is out for you, Octavius, but it isn't Imperius Drake.

The Bear shook his formidable head. "You're right, Colonel. Still, I'm convinced there's some kind of connection to our deceased opponent. I want to talk with our geneticist, Dr. 'Odd' Vark. He kept the mad Duck's

31

files and samples. Imperius abandoned them at UUI when I helped him make his hasty forced exit out the window.

Odd's been using the Duck's records and procedures to track Otto's physical and mental status. Fortunately, the Otter seems to have survived the Duck's experiments with nothing worse than a telekinetic ability to 'zap' from place to place and toss stuff and animals around at will." *(See Book 2-The Case of the Spotted Band.)*

The Wolf replied. "Let's get a hold of Otto and Chita, too. Maybe they can shed some light on this."

Octavius trundled back up to the Ursine Lounge where most of the Octavians were still holding forth. He looked around. "It seems we have a joker on our paws. Someone wants us to believe Imperius Drake has returned. That 'Urgent' package contained a real bomb, not a Black Quack. Remember those?"

Chita blanched *(if a spotted cat could blanch)* "Oh I remember alright. Those and the explosive musical eggs that almost wiped out the world's geneticists in Las Vegas. The Duck was truly insane. He tried to kill me off, too. Several times. I finally got him in Egypt."

Otto scrunched up his face and nodded. "Oh yeah! Tell me about him. I guess he did me a favor with his injections but he and that Bigg Baboon were real scourges."

(As I noted above, an unintended result of the Duck's experiments has turned Otto into a full-fledged telekinetic, able to "zap" from location to location and move objects and individuals almost at will. He needs a surge of adrenaline to trigger the process but is seldom without it. He has a dramatic "fight or flight" capability that has gotten him out of many tight situations. See Book 12- The Nut Case.) He also performs with Belinda's Aquabears, providing slapstick comic relief to their formalized routines.)

He asked, "What's going on, Octavius?"

"Not sure, but I'll bet that package wasn't an isolated shot. I'm sure there's more coming.

Belinda shooed the Cubs off into the kitchens and looked at Octavius. "When did you hire Sedgewick?"

"A few weeks ago, right after you went back over to the Shetlands. I got a call from an employment agency for domestics responding to a request from Frau Schuylkill. She's been at me to get a Butler on staff here at the Lair. Unlike Polar Paradise, we haven't had one. Sedgewick seemed well qualified and personable. So I hired him. Why?"

"Well, he's the only one who saw the animal who brought the package and he couldn't shed any light on the messenger or the car. Was there really a messenger at all?"

"Hey, Bel. Don't go paranoid. Alright, Let's keep an eye on our new domestic but I think you're off base. Remember, in all the detective stories, the Butler never does it."

The Bearoness laughed but raised her residual eyebrows. "I wonder. I think I want to chat with the Frau."

"Do that. See what her current opinion of the Alpaca is."

"What are you going to do?"

"I'm going over to UUI to check the Imperius files with Doctor Vark. Maybe we can find something to shed a little light on this mystery. The Duck has not returned. That's for certain but someone wants us to think so. Can you give me a lift, Colonel?"

Wyatt nodded and got ready for a ride across the river.

They headed for an oversized pickup truck and took off.

On the way over the bridge, Wyatt asked, "What do you expect to get out of that crazy Duck's files? They're probably chock full of mad ramblings and pseudo-science."

"Don't underestimate him. He was nutty as the proverbial fruitcake but he did still have a brilliant mind buried under those layers of psychoses. It's a shame the scientific community didn't originally take Yu-Aul-Kum more seriously. He might have been an influence for good."

"Oh come on, Octavius. Are you getting soft on him?"

"Hardly! That serum of his changed him into Imperius Drake, a raving lunatic, but he wouldn't have been the first scientist who succumbed to his own experimentation. Try Doctor Jerky and Mr. Hype. After I frustrated his use of UUI's lab facilities, Imperius singled me out for major hostility and even death. I had no regret when Chita did him in at the Egyptian tomb. To answer your original question, I'm looking to see who in his vast array of contacts might still be active and seeking revenge on me."

"After all this time?"

"Vengeance is often served cold."

"I think I've heard that before."

"Probably. I don't say much that's original."

"You're sure Bigg Baboon is also dead and gone?"

"Absolutely. Raamjet the Uraeus dropped a stone wall and ceiling on him. Otto saw the body and can attest to his demise. He was smart enough to fire off the Duck's ray gun but he lacked the brains to design and build bombs. No, this isn't Bigg's work. *(See Book 5 – The Curse of the Mummy's Case)*

"What about the Hyena?

"He's caught up in the bowels of an Egyptian underworld along with King Tsk VI and his minions. Sent there forever by the god Anubis. He also has a broken back. No, he's not our villain. And Chita certainly killed off Imperius. We have to look elsewhere. That crazy Duck had contacts all over the world. Remember the Taurus Brothers in Chicago?"

"Yeah, but they're not around anymore either. This is someone new but what his or her motivation is, I don't know."

"I'm more interested in what his, her or their intentions are."

"Certainly nothing felicitous in spite of the message."

The Colonel pulled the truck up to the impressive UUI entrance. He growled. "We're here. Does Vark know you're coming?"

"I called him before we set out. He should have the files ready and waiting."

They parked and then went up to the medical wing.

Chapter Two

The strange Aardvark has claws that are strong.
And his tongue stretches ever so long.
Thus he gobbles up bugs,
Loads of insects and slugs,
But I still think his nose is all wrong.

"They're missing! When you called I went to the files to check and all of his original papers, disks and thumb drives are gone."

Doctor 'Odd' Vark shouted from his office file room. "I haven't looked at the stuff in a while. Once I was convinced Otto was not going to suffer any ill effects from the Duck's experiments, I put the materials away. His serums are still locked up in my safe but the files have disappeared."

Octavius was upset. "Weren't the file cabinets locked?"

"They still are! There are several keys because we share materials. A lot of folks come through this area."

The Colonel asked, "Could someone on your staff be using them?"

"I checked. No one claims to have them. There were four large file folders. Hard to misplace. I did make electronic copies and they're out on the Cloud. Ursula may have a version, too. Ask her! What's going on?"

"Damned if I know! Someone pretending to be Imperius Drake and planting a bomb to prove it. Chita, Otto, Ursula and Wyatt here will be heading out to St. Louis shortly to see if the Duck's laboratory is still standing. It was a shambles the last time we looked and no one has taken up residence since that we know of. That was almost two years ago. I don't think we'll get anything useful out of this trip but I guess it's worth a try. Meanwhile, Dr. Vark, let's you and I do some more searching here at UUI."

*****

36

A UUI helicopter hovered low over the confluence of the Missouri and Mississippi Rivers at Pelican Island near St. Louis, site of the late and unlamented Imperius Drake's former laboratory and headquarters.

"Ursula, it looks deserted from here. Can you check?"

Looks can be deceiving, Colonel. I suggest we land and do an on-site inspection. It seems to be locked up but it looks like it's been somewhat vandalized. Graffiti on the one or two visible surfaces. Most of it is underground. You two remember it, don't you?"

Otto let out a deep breath and shrugged. "Oh, yeah. I remember. Déjà vu, all over again! Shots in the tail to make me a theatrical sensation. That creep!"

Chita winced. "To think I worked for him. Of course, the last time I was in there, I tried to brain him with a heavy glass retort. Did some real damage, too. OK, let's land and see what's what. I wonder if the security systems are still working. But that shouldn't be much of an issue for our AGI friend here."

 Ursula chortled. "No, I don't suppose so. We'll see, shall we!"

Wyatt touched the chopper down carefully in a clearing away from the building. If there was anyone on the island at that moment they were out of sight. The team debarked and worked their way cautiously through the underbrush. They came up on a gravel ramp that led down to a steel door set in concrete. The Duck's semi-submerged lab and HQ. Chita winced with remembrances.

Ursula said, "I doubt the electrical system is still active. Let me try a little legerdemain on the doors."

Lo and behold, the steel blast door rose.

"How did you do that without power?"

"I didn't. The circuits are active. Someone has been here recently. I don't sense them right now but this place has been in use and may be used again. Don't move. There are booby traps set. Let me go to work here."

Flashes! Snaps and crashes! Grinding whines! Dull thuds!

"OK! That takes care of that. You can move in now."

Otto zapped in, passed a locked door, stopped, came back and pulled it open. A large carton of what looked like Black Quacks sat on top of a steel table. "These little beauties are just waiting to be activated. But these models have switches. They're not vintage Imperius. Still, I don't want to tamper with them. What do you think, Colonel? Should we dump them in the river?"

"Why not! We're no surprise anymore! Whoever has taken over here will know someone invaded the place when they find the booby traps dismantled. Might as well remove the eggs and reduce the potential damage. Let's take them but be careful. If they're Black Quacks Model II, they'll blow your ears out if they sound off. If they're bombs, they blow everything off. What else is there, Otto?"

"Not much. The Duck once had a pretty elaborate lab in here but all of that seems to be gone. Probably took the stuff to Egypt with him. There are still the power units and the security system; a couple of beds. This closet has some office supplies and there's a fridge with very stale snacks and some canned drinks. Nothing substantial. Whoever is working here is probably finished but might be coming back to pick up those eggs. But to do what with them?"

"I don't know. Any thoughts. Ursula?"

"Too little data, Colonel. I doubt if they'll be back soon. Could be staying at a nearby hotel. Looks like they come and go by boat. There are signs of a tie-down on the river side dock."

"If it wasn't for those crazy eggs, I might be tempted to say this place has nothing to do with what's happening back at Cincinnati and UUI. Anyway, not much point in hanging around. Let's seal this spot back up, get back in the chopper, fly over the middle of the river and ditch these eggs. That should have our mystery guest puzzled. He'll be wondering what happened to his (or her) Black Quacks? *(If they are Black Quacks.)*"

Otto took one last look around. "Boy, this joint sure brings back memories. None of them very pleasant. *(He rubbed his bottom.)* Those nutty experiments. That dope Bigg! Chita, do you remember sinking the Lee-Li-Li with a pile of rocks. That black hydroplane was the Duck's pride and joy."

Chita howled, "Oh, I remember! Too many memories. I remember bashing him with a heavy bottle and sending him to the hospital. Sorry I didn't kill him then instead of later in Egypt. Oh, let's get the hell out of here. This place is giving me the creeps. Much as I hate helicopters, let's fly, Colonel. Back to Cincy! I could use some champagne."

They crept back to the clearing gingerly carrying the black eggs. Chita took one last look around, shook her head and then clambered aboard the chopper. Otto zapped into his seat. Ursula was doing navigation duty and called up Lambert International Airport to announce their intentions. The Colonel pulled the throttles, revved up the engines, adjusted the cyclic and collective controls and they were airborne.

A brief hovering stop over the Mississippi to dump their load of nasty eggs and they headed east. Back to Cincinnati. It was tough to talk over the sound of the engines and rotors, even with headsets. The Colonel was taken up with flying the chopper. But Ursula was plugged into the comm system and asked: "You two knew Imperius Drake. Do you believe he survived Egypt and is back?"

Otto answered first. "The only way he could be back is if the Egyptian gods rescued him from the Underworld. I find that very hard to believe. However, if they just got around to it that might explain why he took so long to announce his reappearance. But why would they do that? Imperius was clearly an enemy of the gods as was Tsk VI. Very doubtful, Ursula. What do you think, Chita?"

"I left him scattered in little burned out pieces all over that tomb. It would take a very powerful deity to put him back together. Certainly more than 'all the king's lions and all the king's crocs.' Nah, he's gone, Ursula. This is someone else. Or several someones. I wish I knew who."

Otto had kept an egg. Chita asked, "Keeping a souvenir, my little pal?"

"Sort of. I really don't want any more mementos of that nutty bird but I think I want to give this to Octavius. He can add it to his office collection."

"I'm sure he'll be thrilled. I hope the champagne is chilled."

*****

Hi! Maury here again. While Chita and the other intrepid investigators were chewing up the sky on their way back to Cincinnati and the well chilled champagne, another spotted cat approached the Bear's Lair. No, not Cyd, Chita's alleged sister. *(We never did confirm that she really existed.)* And not Jake, Chita's musical drum solo collaborator from the now defunct Spotted Band *(See Book 2 – The Case of the Spotted Band)*

This is yet another fabulous feline - Jaguar Jack the Lad – the most elegant and incorrigible dude on four paws. Truly a Big Cat! Jack gives new meaning to the word 'swashbuckling' with his flamboyant patterned pelt, deep throated roar and swaggering strut. And he's a long standing compadre of Octavius.

It's not clear how they ever got together. The Great Bear has a talent for attracting one-of-a-kinds. And Jack is certainly a singleton. I think the Jaguar came to the Bear's rescue while he was stopping a bank robbery. I never did get the full story but when they get together, they fall into paroxysms of mysterious laughter that they can't or won't explain.

Jack has inexhaustible capacity for tequila. I keep a special locked cellar of different wines and liquors for Octavius' guests. Jack has a special shelf all his own stocked with special Anejo firewater. No doubt he will put a hole in that array.

You'd think a big spotted Jaguar cat would drive a Jaguar, wouldn't you? Not our Jack. His car is a tawny Maserati dotted with black rosettes matching his personality and appearance. It too, had a flamboyant pelt, a swaggering strut and a deep throated roar. In fact, the engine announced his arrival. Sedgewick headed for the mansion's door but I beat him to it. "I'll get it. I know this one, Sedge. He's an old buddy!"

I waved him in. "Hey, Jack. Good to see ya. Come on in. Who's after you this time? The police; a jealous mate out for your blood; a furious senorita; a bunch of angry bookies; a victimized savings and loan; all of the above?"

"Hola, my little compadre. Once again, you do me great wrong. I am tame as a pussycat but I admit I have come to consult El Gran Oso on a matter of some urgency."

"Octavius isn't here at the moment but I expect him back shortly. He's over at UUI. Meanwhile, I'll rustle up a shot or two of tequila. What's the problem?"

"Your Deep Data Hexagon is the problem or actually that Caleb Cassowary is the problem. He's the Chief Technical Officer of the Advanced Super Computing Center. Do you know him?"

"Oh yeah, I know him. A supercilious pain in the ass."

"Well, I think you know I've come up with a Deep Data analysis process for handicapping horse races. Your data analysts are under contract to me."

"How is that working out?"

"Monumental! Although I have to resolve some issues with the Racing Associations. The process was performing beautifully until that Aussie bird pulled the analysts off the project. Higher priorities! Ay Caramba! That's why I'm here. To invoke a little executive suite pressure to get my support team back."

"There isn't much love lost between Octavius and Caleb. I'm sure the Boss will straighten it out as soon as he gets back. Meanwhile, I assume you're staying away from banks and mated senoras."

"Of course, my little amigo! Of course! How about another round of tequilas in the meantime?"

Chita

Chapter Three

So our Ursula just disappeared
In a manner that's really quite weird.
Is her vanishing real
Or a sleight-of-hand deal?
Has she gone for good; much as we feared?

Otto, Wyatt, Chita and Ursula were back from their trip to St. Louis in the UUI chopper.

"So, besides a joy ride over our nation's Midwest, what did you guys accomplish?" Octavius had also returned to the Bear's Lair from his session with Doctor Vark, found nothing and was at his acerbic best. I had told him of Jaguar Jack's arrival. He said he recognized the car in the courtyard. Jack was stretched out snoozing in the Ursine Lounge after imbibing X number of tequilas. "I'll see him shortly."

Otto cried. "Here! Catch!" and tossed the ersatz Black Quack to the Great Bear who bobbled it before clutching it in his oversized paws. I moved out of the way and got ready to run.

"Don't worry, Maury, it's not active. These come equipped with a switch - a model upgrade over the original Imperius version. I kept one to show you and to give to Octavius as a keepsake. We dumped a bunch of them in the muddy Mississippi."

The Colonel added, "The Mad Duck's lab is still there, much the worse for wear. But the power and security systems are functional. Someone has been working there lately but not staying on. Someone who is sophisticated enough to create booby traps and construct these eggs. Someone, I suspect, who doesn't like you very much and has a memory of Imperius Drake. Any ideas?"

"Nobody and anybody!"

Well, that was certainly helpful. He was as much in the dark as we were. I issued the Octavius standby reply. "Hmmm!"

*****

Belinda and the Cubs were listening in. "Momma, is that nasty Duck coming after us?"

"No, dear, he's gone for good. He died in Egypt. You were there."

"Well, who is the Colonel and Otto talking about?

"I don't know. Somebody new!"

"Do you know, Aunt Chita?"

"No, young one. I don't."

"How about you, Ursula?"

No response. Dark screen!

"Ursula?? Aunt Ursie? Momma, why isn't she answering?"

"I don't know, Arabella. Tavi, is Ursula offline?"

"I don't think so. Colonel, see if you can raise her on your unit."

"Nothing. How about you, Otto?"

"No response. I'll check with Howard. " (A pawse.)

"Howard doesn't have anything, either. Very strange."

"Maury, call tech support. She's never disappeared like that before."

The Great Bear gave out one of his famous 'Hmmms' The inevitable followed. "Get on this, Maury. We need her back immediately. Even if the server farm at the Hexagon is out of action, Ursula is not supposed to go down. She is independent and self-powered. This is intolerable."

I checked. The server farm was not out of action. In fact, all things technological were AOK, except for our Universal Ursine Intellect Model 12 – Artificial General Intelligence System. She was gone!

This was a new first. Ursulas were rock-solid and more trustworthy than anybody – forgive me, than any entity. They are isolated from the rest of the systems. Power outages; hackers; conflagrations have no effect. They're almost impossible to turn off. They don't just disappear.

Fail-safe is a much maligned term. "Nothing can go wrong…go wrong…go wrong." But Ursula, especially this latest model comes pretty darn close. She has been in service for close to two years and has operated without a noticeable glitch for that entire period. Her predecessor systems were also super reliable. I don't generally care for the management of the Advanced Super Computing Center of UUI but I have to grudgingly bow in their direction for producing such a magnificent series of technological wonders. The developers are superb. So are their products. Ursulas are truly unique.

Their constantly enhanced operational capabilities have been more than matched by their ruggedness, security, multi-layer backup, seamless recovery and self-repair. We are constantly amazed by their functional abilities. Go back to Ursula 12's personal introduction in the Prologue of this book for a refresher on what she is and what she can do. What goes relatively unnoticed is their incredible dependability. It's just assumed at this point.

Well, we just got a jolt. It isn't clear whether she has suffered a fatal blow or has deliberately taken herself offline. But if deliberate, why? It would be a first. They have been known to go into a reduced function protective mode if faced with a threat or a need to reboot which is very seldom. They do self- maintenance in idle periods but until now we have always been aware of what is going on and their status.

This is different. Complete loss of communication. No response at all.

It's as if she didn't exist. That of course, is patently ridiculous. We are all too familiar with her chime calling for our attention and the variety of faces and voices she presents to her "adoring public." Series 12 has a unique temperament. Of all the Ursulas, she has a personality that reeks independence.

The Ursulas were never intended to be "purpose built" robots tied to a prescribed set of functions. The "G" in their AGI nomenclature stands for 'General' but unlike her predecessors, Ursula 12 has taken on a degree of autonomy that exceeds all of our expectations. Ursie is different and number 13 when she emerges bodes well to be even more of a conundrum. Nobody is sure how they will develop. We shall see. However, our current task is to find the elusive number 12. My current task!

There are times when Octavius can be overbearing. *(No pun intended.)* This is one of them. Who was that starship captain who used to say, "Make it so"? I don't think he was a bear but he could have been. "Maury, see to it!" Sure, Octavius!

Something was awry as they say in the adventure books and I was stuck with finding out what that something was. I kept hoping she would just reappear but so far, no such luck. Oh well, I get all the impossible jobs. Looks like a job for Super-Maury! First some fermented coconut milk VSOP and then the game is apaw.

Maury Meerkat

The Development of Civilization - Volume 13
Part 2
Deep Data–Analyzing Big Data–the Five HV's

From *"An Introduction to Faunapology"*
by *Octavius Bear Ph.D.*

Bytes, kilobytes, megabytes, gigabytes, terabytes, petabytes, exabytes, zettabytes, yottabytes. *(1000 bytes raised to the 8th power.)* Big Data!

Deep Data analysis utilizes advanced techniques on very large, diverse, structured, semi-structured or unstructured data sets. These are often beyond the ability of traditional relational databases to retrieve, secure, manage and process.

Big Data has one or more "HV" attributes: High Volume, High Velocity, High Variety and we hope, through Deep Data analysis, High Veracity and High Value. In a very real sense, bringing order out of chaos is the primary mission of Deep Data processes.

Artificial Intelligence, 5G and the Internet of Things are driving data complexity with new forms and sources of information. Big Data can come from sensors, devices, video/audio, networks, web and social media, transactions and applications —often in real time and on a very large scale.

Big Data is like an informational suction pump. It can collect everything-significant or otherwise. Useful trends can be found in this mass of data, but it's much harder to determine what is useful and what is not. Deep Data techniques propelled by skilled analysts, looks for specific information to help predict trends or make other calculations.

Analysis of Big Data allows enterprises to make better and faster decisions using information that was previously inaccessible or unusable. Major applications like CRM (Customer Relationship Management) can use semantic indexing to organize and retrieve information in more meaningful forms. Businesses, institutions and governments can use advanced Deep Data analytics to gain new insights from previously untapped data sources as well as existing data.

Artificial Intelligence techniques are tied directly to Deep Data analytics.

Developing algorithms that perform very large scale, discriminatory activities on Big Data, separating useful information and trends from noise, is the responsibility of a select team of highly skilled analysts. They, in turn, rely on state of the art technology to advance their undertakings.

The UUI Advanced Super Computing Center has taken a worldwide lead in this exciting and highly demanding environment, contributing heavily to new research and development while making extensive investments in management, staff and infrastructure. We are pushing the data analytic envelope dramatically. In turn, we expect Big and Deep Data to be major sources of revenue growth for the foreseeable future.

Chapter Four

And over the hillsides I go
To meet the Great Bear's CTO
What a frustrating quest!
He's an arrogant pest.
Just not someone I've wanted to know!

OK! Where is she? I checked with everyone who had an Ursula support device. No joy! No suggestions. If she's hiding, she's doing a hell of a job. If she's "dead" we have a major dilemma on our paws.

Next stop: Her birthplace and home, the Advanced Super Computing Center of UUI. A Jeep ride away in the Kentucky hills. Off we went. While soaking up the scenery, I kept trying to get my paws around what was up with Ursula 12. I kept drawing blanks.

Suddenly, a huge building loomed out of the woods. My driver pulled up and gave me a full view of the Big Data Hexagon. Octavius had poured tons of money into the project. So far, it was paying off beautifully.

Envision a mile-square, four story, six sided, copper colored structure capped with antennas, a heliport and solar panel arrays and surrounded by wind turbines and extensive parking lots. *(The Pentagon on steroids.)*

The bottom two stories are taken up with power supplies feeding the insatiable demands of the main frames, servers and quantum computing units that occupy the third floor. The top floor is mostly open plan with work and gathering spaces where designers, developers, programmers, coders, data analysts, cloud and artificial intelligence support teams ply their respective trades. Tucked away in one wing is a column of offices assigned to the Hex management brains.

In the biggest of those offices sits the extremely brilliant but extremely caustic Caleb Cassowary – the Center's Chief Technical

Officer. Not for him, the mundane IT functions of UUI's day-to-day operations. Those belong to Martin Marten, the CIO who is housed in the main UUI complex back near the Ohio river. Caleb lives out here in the rarified atmosphere of the true information illuminati - thinking and speaking thoughts and languages known exclusively to a highly select few. His ideas fly over the heads of even the most experienced and acknowledged data experts. In short, he is an info super snob and classic pain in the tail.

I have been granted the privilege of approaching him, not through any personal merit but rather because of my association with the Great Bear whom Caleb grudgingly acknowledges as his employer.

"Well, Meerkat, what is your problem with Ursula 12? Do you and your Boss have some difficulty with my sublime protégé? Is she not performing to your exacting specifications?"

"Your sublime protégé has disappeared! She's been off the grid for over eight hours. Our folks and your folks can't find her." Watching his yellow eyes pop and his head casque wobble was worth the price of admission.

Southern Cassowaries are daunting avians, at the best of times. They are known as the most dangerous birds in the world. Caleb is a 24 carat example. He's over six feet in length, flightless, covered in black and dark blue feathers. Formidable beak, double wattles.

The Australian accent puts me in mind of my buddy, Bruce Wallaroo, but that's where the resemblance ends. Bruce is a chum. Caleb is a chump. But just don't mess with those fearsome claws. His legs are like trees and one kick is all it takes to polish off an opponent. Fortunately *(or unfortunately)* this guy relies on his formidable intellect rather than his footwork. I guess that's a plus. I could see he was perplexed. What had happened to Ursula 12?

"Obviously, an exogenous infrastructure failure."

"What infrastructure? She's totally self-contained. How else could she travel in the Multiverse? I realize you don't think much of my opinions but I think she's gone rogue!"

"That is categorically impossible. Her independence is conditioned by highly sophisticated values, vectors and algorithms that would inhibit any such activity. Ursula doesn't know how to rebel."

"You tell her that…if you can find her!"

"Oh, we'll find her and when we do you will regret your doubts about her. Ursula is about as close to perfection as is possible."

"OK. I have lived and worked with Ursulas for quite a while. I am extremely impressed and actually quite fond of them. But, just be assured that as of the moment, Octavius Bear, our mutual employer, is not convinced of her perfection and is not very happy. I think it's in both our interests to improve his frame of mind."

He stared at me. "I know you consider yourself to be a skilled detective. Meerkat. That is laughable. Ursula can outwit you and those other incompetents Octavius has on his staff without raising a microvolt of her energy. What are you all called? Octavians? More like Octogenarians. She is my brainchild and newer versions are on the way. Ursula 13 will be even more formidable."

"Well, Caleb, right now your brainchild has taken a bunk and in the interest if of keeping your job, you need to bring her back."

"Don't try to intimidate me, you Kalahari pipsqueak. You and your Boss are a pair of swaggerers whose intellects aren't in the same universe as mine. Go back and tell him Ursula 12 will be back in service shortly.."

(It's tough for a two-foot tall meerkat to make a dramatic exit but I flourished my tail, executed a sharp 180° turn and stomped out leaving the Big Bird staring pensively. I was on my way back to the Bear's Lair and another fermented coconut milk VSOP. He was trying to figure out where the AGI had gotten to.)

Chapter Five

I'm not sure that I know what to do.
I'm afraid that the rumor is true.
I admit with a frown
That we all have come down
With a case of severe Déjà Vu.

(The Ursine Lounge)

Jaguar Jack the Lad looked over at Octavius and sighed. "It sounds to me as if my pressing issue is going to take second place to your deadly conundrum. I have a problem with your Hexagon Data folks. As you know, I have invented a Deep Data process for handicapping horse races and your analysts have been working with me…until now. That smart-ass CTO of yours has pulled them off the project. Higher priorities! Carajo! That's why I'm here. To invoke a little executive suite pressure to get my support team back. But I gather you're being threatened by some jerk who wants to resuscitate Imperius Drake and do you in. Just like the old days, Octavius! Déjà Vu."

Up to this point, Condo had been observing all, but saying little. Quietly sitting in the lounge, huge wings folded around him, a glass of Scotch in one of his claws, he gave off an air of studied pensiveness. Then he looked around and exercising his technically augmented voice box, squawked in frustration. "Just what the hell is going on here? None of this is making any sense. Senhor Bear, I can understand yet another assassination attempt on you. You're a rich, powerful ursine who has made an immense amount of money and more than his fair share of enemies. I suppose you have to expect the occasional incursion against you although I'm sure you don't welcome it. But what's all this stuff about the loony Duck? Imperius Drake Revisited?"

The Bear stared at the Condor. "I'm not sure I feel all that philosophical about being a target, Senhor, but I can't shed any light on your question. As far as I'm concerned, Imperius Drake is a dead letter item - no pun intended. I don't know about the bomb or who made his notes disappear or why and I certainly have no clue as to the resumed activity in his former lab. Some assassin has a Duck fetish. Imperius is a symbol."

The Bird said. "Is he immortal? I thought I'd gotten rid of him over the Ohio River and again in Egypt. Are we certain he's passed on? Did you really kill him, Chita?"

The Cat chirped, "Yes, Condo, I actually disassembled him with a ray gun. But you may have hit on it, Bear. Symbolism. Replaying the Bear-Duck war in hopes the results will turn out differently this time. Someone knows the Duck's sick history and is intent on regurgitating it. We were all a party to it. We may all be targets. You, Belinda, Otto, Maury, Wyatt, Ilse, Condo, Howard, Me, Even Odd Vark and Chiti BingBang. Did somebody say Bruce Wallaroo was coming up from Aussie-land? Him too. All of us! Anyway, you got it, Otto. It's good old déjà vu, all over again."

The otter squeaked. "So what do we do? Wait for the next bomb? No thanks! And what's the story with Ursula? Did you get any satisfaction out of your session with the CTO, Maury?"

"Arrogant as usual! He wouldn't admit it but he's flummoxed, too. Not sure what he's going to do. Probably trouble-shooting, beating up on his staff, and running all sorts of diagnostics but I believe our Ursula has deliberately gone incommunicado. If she doesn't want to be found, she won't be found. I haven't the slightest idea why she's behaving that way but that AGI has depths no one has explored including her so-called makers. She's the twelfth of her kind. Who knows what squirrely code has evolved over time to create her current personalities. She'll probably come back when she's damned good and ready. Meanwhile, we make do."

That didn't sit well with Octavius who was just beginning to realize how much we have come to depend on Ursula. He picked up his oversized smart phone. "Get me Caleb Cassowary. Thanks! *(a pawse)* Caleb? Octavius Bear. What's the story with Ursula? No, I don't want the reasons. I want results. Her backup isn't working? Well, bring up one of the earlier versions. You did keep them in reserve, I hope. OK. We'll be waiting. Not very patiently, I might add. Thanks."

A minute went by and a flash lit up the laptops in the Ursine Lounge. A gargling voice sounded out. "Hello, I'm Universal Ursine Ursula Model 11. Please stand by while I restart and perform self-diagnostics. Thank you."

Her speech changed into a more pleasant and familiar pattern. "I'm fully operational now. How may I be of service?"

Otto asked the same question on all our minds. "You're number 11? What's happened to our current Model 12?"

"I'm sorry. I've been in retirement. I only have knowledge of my predecessor systems. Is there a Model 12?"

Octavius retorted, "Yes there is! So you don't have any recollection of 12's most recent activities and inputs."

"No, I don't. You may want to go out to the Cloud and summon her backup."

"Already done that. It's blocked."

"That's very strange. Do you have proper authorization?"

I thought Octavius was going to hit the roof. "I'm Octavius Bear and I have total authorization for all UUI systems and subsystems. I'm telling you Ursula 12's backup is blocked. Tell Cassowary to get her files freed up immediately."

"Yes Doctor Bear. May I have your password, please?"

Ouch!! I'll pass over the ensuing noisy tirade resulting from that request. At the best of times, Octavius' patience is in short supply. This was not the best of times. Number 11 did manage to supply some basic services but it was hardly satisfactory. Where the hell is Number 12? Her backup files are missing and so is she. She's hiding! Why?

I didn't have a clue. My session with Caleb Cassowary had proven to be fruitless or worse and so far, the Hexagon staff had done nothing to solve the issue. I decided to call his aide, Byzantia. The Bonobo may indeed be the true brains of the Hexagon. She is certainly easier to deal with than Caleb.

She too expressed total puzzlement. She said this was totally out of character for an Ursula. They were working on it but so far, no results.

Byzz sounded as if she had something else she wanted to discuss but changed her mind.   I will have to spend some more time communicating with her away from Caleb. But not now.

The Development of Civilization -Volume 13 - Part 3

5G - Fifth Generation Cellular Technology

From "An Introduction to Faunapology"
by Octavius Bear Ph.D.

Sometime in the future we may be casually referring to "n" generation communication technology. Right now, 5G is the cellular buzzword du jour. Yes, there were (and still are) generations 1 through 4. We won't take time to describe them, however. 4G is our current usage base and is, at least in the US, the cellular workhorse. Some countries are further back in cellular development. A few are ahead.

5G, the new fifth generation technology standard for cellular networks, brings with it three new plusses: larger channel bandwidth (to speed up data movement), lower latency (faster response times) and the ability to connect many more and varied devices at once (e.g. sensors and smart devices).

In addition to raw speed, one of the key benefits of 5G is low latency. Latency is the response time when you click on a link or start streaming a video. "I don't want to wait!" These activities send the request up to the network, and when the network responds, delivers the desired website or plays your video. Low latency means fast turnaround.

The 5G network is designed to connect a far greater number and variety of devices than our current cellular network. You've heard of IoT, the Internet of Things? Right now, more gadgets communicate over the Internet than do people. 5G can power multiple devices of all types and support a much wider range of applications. The 5G network can adjust for differing hardware and software needs.

So 5G networks will not just serve cellphones but could also be used as general internet service providers (ISPs) for laptops and desktop computers; make possible new applications in the Internet of Things (IoT) and machine to machine connections. By the way, current 4G cellphones will not be able to use the new networks, which will require new 5G enabled wireless devices.

Like their predecessors, 5G networks are cellular. Their service areas are divided into small geographical spaces called cells. All the 5G wireless devices in a cell are connected to the Internet and telephone network by radio waves through a local antenna. The antennas are usually but not always attached to towers. In cities, high rise buildings may substitute.

5G gets most of its increased speed by using higher frequency radio waves than current cellular networks. A lot of the higher frequencies are currently unused but will soon be pressed into service. However, higher-frequency radio waves have a shorter range than those used by previous cell phone implementations. This results in many more, smaller individual cellular zones requiring more antennas and towers to support the same service areas.

To offset this increase and ensure wide coverage, 5G networks operate on up to three distinct frequency bands, low, medium, and high. Each requires different antennas, trading off speed vs. distance and service area size. Not all 5G environments will offer the same service levels to all customers and users. Obviously, this will impact infrastructure decisions and user costs. Travelers may encounter more differences in service as they move from location to location. Not all devices will support all three modes.

Beyond supplying a big speed boost, 5G is fundamentally innovative and futuristic. It will eventually provide such capabilities as support for self-driving cars and other vehicles; virtual and augmented reality and telemedicine services like remote surgery. Look for transformation in education methods. Banking and money transfer are changing. The phone is displacing the credit card which in turn displaced cash. 5G is coming. But at what pace? Who knows exactly? In some cases, it's already here. It will eventually connect everything from farming equipment to security cameras and, of course, your smartphone.

Will there be a 6G? Probably, but not for quite a while!

UUI is heavily into 5G as well as Big / Deep Data and Clouds. We, like other network providers, are committed to offering maximum telecommunication and information processing capabilities to all of our clients.

Chapter Six

The species that's called Wallaroo
Is a wallaby plus kangaroo.
His large feet - (macropod!)
Make him look rather odd
But I bet he moves faster than you.

Maury here once again. I had turned back to the Great Bear just in time to watch him keel over. His narcolepsy had kicked in. Possibly because of his current frustration. His sleep disorder comes about as a result of his successful genetic efforts to avoid having to hibernate. He denies having the narcoleptic problem but the Octavians know better. Belinda thinks it's rather amusing as long as he doesn't get hurt. The Cubs don't know what to make of it. Anyway, he'll be back shortly. The sleep episodes are usually short-lived. Meanwhile, he snored on.

Anyway, when this Imperius nonsense first surfaced, I placed a call to Chief Inspector Bruce Wallaroo who shares a Duck-fighting history with Octavius Bear. He is currently on assignment from Australia to Interpol in Lyon, France.

At my request, Bruce took a short leave and snagged a flight to Cincinnati on Belinda's Concorde with the Flying Tigers in command. That aircraft has been doing yeoman duty shuttling Octavian players hither and yon and reducing the size of the Bear's fabulous wealth in the process. Operating and maintaining the Ursine Air Force is a major financial drain but neither Octavius nor Belinda will hear of reducing or stinting on the expense. I recently got a raise so who am I to complain.

It turned out that we were to have other visitors. In the interval since Belinda returned to the States, the exiled king of Dalmatia had passed away but the assassins were still threatening Lord David the Chamberlain. He called and wondered if the Bearoness' gracious offer to give him and his Boxer bodyguard shelter was still available. It was and Belinda arranged for the Flying Tigers on their return from Lyon to take the C-5A Ursa Major to the UK and pick up the Dalmatian dog *(more spots!)* the Boxer and his beloved fire engine. Dougal was coming over from Polar Paradise to help celebrate the twins' fourth birthday. The white Bengals were logging in plenty of flight time.

While we waited for the Wallaroo to arrive, the Twins, who adore him, kept up a steady stream of "Is he here yets?" Mlle Woof took it upon herself to suggest a diversion. "Mes Petits, let us see if Frau Ilse could take us on the Belinda B. for a short trip up the Ohio River. When we get back, Uncle Bruce will probably have arrived."

The Belinda B. is a small paddle wheel steamer originally purchased by the Great Bear as a wedding gift for the Bearoness. At the end of Book 2 – *The Case of the Spotted Band,* the dastardly Bigg Baboon scuttled the boat in an effort to kill off Chita who was hiding aboard at the time. Otto saved her and both Imperius and Bigg took off in further pursuit of their rotten ways.

In any event, the Belinda B. has been refloated, refitted and serves once again as a fun source of diversion for the Octavians, especially the Cubs. The boat was to be used for the Cubs' birthday party tomorrow. Frau Schuylkill, or I should say, Kapitän Ilse Schuylkill skippers the boat and as usual cannot deny Arabella and McTavish anything. Off they went on their river cruise. Mlle Woof, although not very fond of water, came along for the ride and to supervise the Furballs.

*****

Once again, the sound of whining jets was heard in the courtyard of the Bear's Lair. The Concorde SST! The Flying Tigers taxied up and maneuvered the Aquabear into position in front of the Romanesque hangar and shut down the engines. As the ground crew rolled up the airstairs, the fuselage door opened and two oversized marsupial feet stomped impatiently. Chief Inspector Bruce Wallaroo of Interpol had arrived.

Octavius, who was now awake after his short snooze, stood at the base of the stairs and held out his giant paws in greeting.

"Good to have you back. old friend. We have some cold Foster's ready for you. How was the trip?"

"Quick and comfortable. I don't know and I don't want to know what it costs to keep that plane flying but one vote for continued Concorde amenities."

"Don't worry. Belinda would rather die than take the Aquabear out of service. It's her pet project. We spend a fortune on maintenance and spare parts but she insists it's worth it. I guess it is. Frankly, I prefer the Ursa Major. More interior room. It will be heading out shortly to pick up the Dalmatian Chamberlain, Lord David, his fire engine and his bodyguard / trainer. We're going to need your help on that one too. Croatian assassins are after him. Always like to keep you busy. C'mon in. Thanks for making the trip. We really have some weird stuff going on. I'll fill you in over a couple of brews. Chita and Jaguar Jack the Lad are here with the Octavians. Big cats galore! The twins are out for a river cruise with Frau Schuylkill but they've been asking for you all day."

"Good on 'em. Be lovely to see them again. Lovely to see you all. G'day Bearoness! G'day Maury! G'day Chita! Hey, Otto! Condo! Colonel! Jaguar Jack. G'day all! Ocko, do I understand you folks employ that notorious Australian bird, Caleb Cassowary?"

"Right! Do you know him?"

"Oh yeah! He made quite a name for himself in Canberra annoying the hell out of all our technology mavens and government dignitaries. Quite a powerful ego, has our fella. He also has a big mouth. Pushy! Gets him in trouble.

"That's a classic understatement."

"He finally read the handwriting on the wall and decided to migrate to the States before he got thrown out of Australia. I didn't realize he had landed here. Lucky you."

"He's a thorn in many of our sides but he is something of a genius."

"That's what he'd like you to believe."

"You don't think so?"

"I'm dubious but who am I to judge. What's this Imperius hoo-hah?"

"That's what we'd all like to know. I thought you'd be interested."

"Actually, I live in hope of never having to think of that Drongo Duck again. He is dead, isn't he?"

Chita snarled. "Oh, he's dead alright. I saw to that. Somebody is pretending to be him. They have a very warped sense of humor including sending a bomb."

"Crikey, that's anti-social! Any idea who?"

"Not a clue. Hoping you can give us a paw."

"Well, that's what we policemen are supposed to do. Bring me up to speed on both situations. Or should I wait to talk to the spotted dog directly when he arrives?"

"Let's deal with the Imperius issue first."

We told him about the egg-bombs and the apparent re-use of the Duck's Mississippi Lab. Three beers and a half hour later, Bruce shook his head. "This is just beginning. Someone's got it in for you, Ocko. Actually, they've got it in for all of us."

Otto squeaked, "Too right, Inspector. Imperius had connections all over the world. Some of them are still alive. And don't discount any off-world players. Imperius hadn't been all that big on the Multiverse but that doesn't mean some of them might not be itching to get back at Octavius for any number of slights, real or imagined. How about those crazy avians on Biosphere X?"

"Did Imperius really have any friends? He threatened everyone he dealt with."

"He may not have had friends but some of those bad actors really had it in for Octavius."

"I guess you're right. Fortunately, most of them are dead. There are still one or two of them who could be a menace plus the paranoid birds on that exoplanet."

"If it's tied to Imperius, I don't understand the timing. Why wait a couple of years to take out vengeance?"

The Wallaroo replied, "It might not be vengeance. This whole thing may be a smokescreen for something altogether different."

'Smokescreen' was the magic word. Just then, an alarm bell clanged and a god-awful horn blatted out repeatedly.

Wyatt jumped up. "It's a fire alarm. It's coming from the hangar. Come on!" The room emptied and we ran out the massive mansion doors.

Flames were shooting up outside one wall of the hangar. Nothing else seemed to be touched. The ground crew had an extinguisher aimed at the blaze and were having some success in putting it out. Thank goodness there had been no explosions. The SST was still standing outside the hangar and the C-5A was sitting on the taxiway waiting for clearance for its trip to Old Blighty. The rest of the aircraft in the hangar as well as the offices and maintenance shops were unaffected.

A gasoline fire? An accident? It seemed to be restricted to the avgas pump used by the propeller aircraft and helicopters. The jet fuel wasn't touched.

Had our mystery opponent struck again? We needed to dig into this.

What are the connections in all of these incidents? A bomb, missing files, a gasoline fire? Is it just harassment or is there some hidden meaning behind it all. Will there be more? I hope not.

Thank goodness the Wallaroo is here to help us along. It's a shame the Chamberlain and his fire engine had not yet arrived. I wonder if he has ever used it to put out blazes. I'll have to ask.

Chapter Seven

On an afternoon cruise without care,
Up the river, just taking the air.
What a paddling delight,
Not a problem in sight!
Then the Cubs get a terrible scare.

(At The Deep Data / Big Data Hexagon)

"Is Sedgewick carrying out his instructions?"

"Yes, but I think this is all a big mistake."

"You are not being paid to think, Byzantia, just act. I'll do the thinking. I am brilliantly qualified to do so as you are well aware."

"Alright, Caleb, but messing with Octavius Bear is a big time risk."

"A risk I am more than prepared to take. Right now, I'm just toying with him. The big blow is yet to fall. It will be devastating when it comes."

"But why??"

"I have reasons of my own. Just do your job. Do you have any news on Ursula 12?"

"Still missing! Not a trace."

"Unsatisfactory. Deal with it. Immediately!"

*****

This dialogue between the CTO of the Advanced Super Computing Center and Byzz, his unappreciated female Bonobo assistant, was taking place while flames were being extinguished at the small avgas pump next to the Bear's Lair gigantic aircraft hangar. Fortunately, the larger jet fuel supply, offices, support equipment and all the aircraft themselves were untouched.

Colonel Where growled. "This looks damned suspicious. A little arson, perhaps. Is our bomb-making friend at it again?"

Octavius looked over at the ground crew. "Any idea how this happened?"

Shrugs! No one saw anything. Spontaneous? Doubtful!

"Wyatt, how about a little forensic investigation,? Can you assist, Bruce? Any evidence of accelerants, incendiary devices?"

"No. Just some spilled aviation gas probably touched off by a spark or a flame. Could have been carelessness but I doubt it. I'm pretty sure it was deliberate. Anyway, it stopped short of starting a conflagration. Thank goodness no one was hurt and no serious damage done."

"Let's get to the bottom of this. This was no accident. Somebody's playing a dangerous game. I'm losing patience here."

The Great Bear was well and truly upset.

*****

Upriver another scenario was being played out. Frau Ilse and two crew members were taking the Cubs and Mlle Woof for a short Ohio River joyride on the Belinda B. A favorite pastime. The plan was to hold the Cubs' birthday party on the boat tomorrow, weather permitting. This was to be a test run.

Oops! Suddenly the cable connecting the two stern rudders to the helm came loose. The paddles kept churning but the steering wheel stopped responding and the boat turned away from the main channel. The Frau stopped the engines but the vessel kept drifting and finally ended up on a sandbar. Stuck!! Verdammt! The Cubs went ballistic. Minus an Ursula, the Frau picked up the ship-to-shore phone and called the Coast Guard and the Bear's Lair.

Otto was first out the mansion door, zapping up the river bank until he came to the paddle steamer. He waved at the Frau, bounded over the stern wheel and called out to the two crewmen to join him. Together they re-shackled the cable back to the rudders. The otter had been called on to repair the boat once again. Another case of sabotage? Shades of Bigg Baboon.

Now they needed to wait for the Coast Guard tug to haul the Belinda B. back into deep water. He inspected under the hull to make sure it was still intact. So far so good. The mischief seemed to be limited to the rudder shackles. The Cubs were beside themselves with excitement. Little did they know what had really happened. "Do it again, Uncle Otto!" Finally, with the arrival of the USCG, the paddle steamer was pulled off the sandbar and back in action.

The Frau was beside herself with irritation. She thanked the Coast Guard and had a special hug for Otto and the crew. The Furballs had an exciting story to tell everyone when they returned home.

"We might have sunk, Momma...but we didn't."

Back at the Lair, Otto, Bel, the Frau, Wyatt, Condo, Jack, Bruce and Octavius all wondered the same thing. How did the rudder shackles come loose? Accident? Unlikely. Wear and tear. Not on a craft supervised by Kapitän Frau Schuylkill! Sabotage? Bingo! But who?

Responding to her personal suspicions, Belinda did a bit of detecting on her own.! She called Octavius over. Call it a sow's intuition. Something about Sedgewick didn't seem legit.

She summoned one of the maids. Sure enough. He had vanished.

"Where is he, Tavi? His room's empty and no one has seen him since morning. Butlers are supposed to be right on the spot. Now that she's back after her harrowing experience, we need to talk with Frau Schuylkill. Where did this guy come from?"

Octavius knew enough not to push back. "I don't know, Bel, but his disappearance might explain a few things."

Ilse had little to add beyond her interaction with a domestic employment agency. Octavius had actually done the interview. Sedgewick seemed to have fine credentials but credentials can be faked. His demeanor was good and he clearly had experience. Where did he really come from and more important, what was his game? Was he working for someone? Who?

*****

Back at the Hexagon, Byzz Bonobo followed up. She determined that Sedgewick had left the Bear's Lair and was on his way out of town to another assignment as a professional disruptor. Caleb should be pleased with his antics but as usual, he wouldn't be. She knew he wouldn't be. Not Caleb.

Byzz shook her head in disgust. If the employment market weren't so tough for female Bonobos *(or for any Bonobos!)* she would tell Caleb what he could do with his job. As it was, she had to suck it up and be the good soldier.

But she was getting to the end of her endurance. This had to stop. His arrogant self-regard was just too much. He was constantly taking advantage of her good nature. And taking on Octavius Bear was sheer folly. What was it that had Caleb so incensed at the Bear? Why his fanaticism about Imperius Drake? Were there solid reasons or was Caleb just a compulsive nut? She'd probably never know.

She needed to find an escape. She had several possibilities but they were all in the future, For the moment she could only play along and act as if she were supporting Caleb. Unfortunately, she actually was supporting Caleb. Her conscience didn't really bother her though. She actually didn't like Octavius Bear. The big Boss. Throwing his money around. That gang of his-the Octavians. Who did they think they were?

She'd never met his wife. The Bearoness with her resort in Scotland and her supersonic airplane. Their Cubs were supposed to be holy terrors. Smart as whips. They invented a million-user Internet game. Something about Brave Bears. Caleb could use them.

That Porcupine and his Dolphin buddy thought they owned Multiverse travel. Little did they know. She and Caleb had some alternate universe surprises in store for them

Those two Wolves might have been a problem. They took security very seriously and were quite good at it. This time, they'd be bypassed.

There was an Otter and a Cheetah. They all had been out to St. Louis and broken into the Duck's lab. They stole and destroyed the lethal eggs that Sedgewick had produced. Probably just as well. Byzz hated those eggs.

Now she found out that fool Jaguar and his horse race handicapping had shown up to get his Deep Data team back. Octavius was sure to throw his massive weight around and Caleb would dump the problem on her. Someone else to give her agita. She wondered if his betting system really worked.

But the one that bothered her the most was that wise-cracking Meerkat. Mauritius. Maury. A two foot tall squirt. He's been bothering her and Caleb about the missing Ursula 12. Those Octavians had a real thing about the Ursulas. They increasingly relied on her. She guessed she was worth it. Byzz had made her what she was. A technological miracle. Caleb, of course, took credit for the series.

Meantime, where the hell is Ursula 12? No one seemed to know. Byzantia certainly didn't. Caleb didn't. That AGI had disappeared and covered her tracks very carefully.

Why? Ursulas by their very nature were designed not to deceive their makers or their owners. This one had gone rogue. A major design flaw. The AGI development team would answer for it. Caleb wouldn't tolerate that sort of failure. Heads would roll but he would do nothing to remedy the situation.

The whole Ursula program was conducted in strict secrecy and limited to a very few high performance designers, developers and technicians. Increasingly, Ursulas were being used to create next generation Ursulas. Was this part of the problem? Were the AGIs becoming too independent? Did the humans know what was going on? She had a vague recollection of the HAL 9000 series in that crazy Space Odyssey story. That turned into a disaster.

The Ursula program needed an in depth review. Caleb wouldn't authorize it, she was sure. His ego wouldn't admit to failure. Byzz would have to do it on the sly. She had access to the devices and development processes that created them. There were a couple of team members who disliked Caleb whom she could trust. She'd have to get started on that analysis right away. If there was a fundamental flaw in the AGI package, she'd have to rectify it quickly and completely.

But meanwhile, Ursula 12 was essential to Caleb's plans. She had to be found.

Chapter Eight

I guess now you've probably heard
Cassowary's a horrible bird.
He's a screwball and threat.
He's a real Space Cadet
And his plans are quite clearly absurd

Narrator's Note:

Caleb Cassowary is an avid avian supremacist. He believes that birds, directly descended as they are from the dinosaurs, have an historic right, priority and obligation to rule. To support his conviction, he has made an extensive study of the late, great Imperius Drake and has studiously endeavored to emulate his every move toward global domination and beyond. His current position as Chief Technical Officer of the Advanced Super Computing Center UUI, has afforded him an outstanding opportunity to exercise his formidable genius in the pursuit of cosmic superiority by exploiting highly sophisticated technology. He has major plans to capitalize on it.

Like his warped predecessor, Caleb harbors an extreme hatred for Octavius Bear and ursines in general. In fact, his animosity extends to most mammalian, reptilian and even some avian species. He also has a special dislike for all the Octavians, especially me.

I don't know why we keep him on. Brilliant or so he would have you believe but he is, after all, one of the world's most dangerous birds. Let's face it, he is a walking feathered calamity. A most perilous character.

Until recently, Caleb's hostilities have been more theoretical than practical. That has begun to change, first with minor sniping against the Bear and his minions. Witness Sedgewick's harassing forays. The egg-bombs. The fire. The paddle boat's sabotage. Early warnings but the Bear wouldn't recognize the signals. Caleb was just playing with him. He'd soon discover how serious the situation was to become.

Now, as a dramatic next step to achieve his ultimate goal of total domination, both in this world and in alternate universes, the CTO is preparing to launch a devastating assault designed to overthrow Octavius and his empire. Imperius Drake would be proud but he was a piker. Caleb's ambitions far outstripped the Duck's.

His outrageous plan is in the final stages of development and with Byzantia Bonobo's assistance, things are falling nicely into place. Just a few more moves to make. Then the world would have Caleb Cassowary to contend with. Like Imperius before him, Caleb had a long list of offenders and offenses to unleash his vengeance upon. Much to do but delightful to consider.

One major glitch – the annoyingly absent Ursula 12. She was a key to his plan. Byzz would have to answer for the breakdown.

He has had to revert to calling up and using Ursula 11. She would have to do. Nothing was going to stop him now. Certainly not a wayward AGI. They were too far along to stop or alter plans.

*****

(The Bear's Lair)

"Maury, have we heard anything from Ursula 12? This Model 11 is driving me nuts. Every time I think she's on top of things, she draws a blank."

"Sorry, Octavius, still nothing. I thought we might hear from the Hexagon but they seem to be at a loss as well."

Condo looked up from yet another bowl of Scotch. "Speaking of the Hexagon, maybe it's just a bird thing on my part, but is anyone else here bothered by this guy Caleb Cassowary?"

I replied, "He's an arrogant, egotistical, condescending pain in the tail but besides that what's bugging you?"

"He reminds me of Imperius Drake."

"Are we all going Imperius daffy? Ever since that egg bomb exploded in the river and we rediscovered that island laboratory, that loony

Duck has been subject number one on every one's agenda. Fuhgeddaboudit! The Damn Duck is dead. Full stop!"

"Sim! I know, but our friend Caleb is very much alive and I don't trust him."

Octavius grinned, "Neither do I. I regret ever putting him in that job. He is brilliant. No doubt about that. But…"

Belinda rolled her eyes. "Maybe that's the problem. Imperius was brilliant, too. Look what happened with him."

"Oh no, Bearoness. Not you, too."

"A sow's intuition, Maury. Caleb's going to be trouble. He is trouble. He and Imperius are very much alike. He even has an ape assistant. Just like Bigg Baboon."

"His assistant is a female Bonobo. Unlike Bigg, she's smart, technically savvy and unaggressive. No comparison. Her name is Byzantia. Many studies indicate that females have a higher status in Bonobo society so it's no surprise she holds a responsible job. What is unique is her extreme technical expertise. I'm willing to bet she's the real brains behind Caleb's professional prowess although he'd never admit it.

Octavius said, "Senhor Condor, let's keep a careful eye on that lady. She may be even more trouble than the Cassowary. I wonder if she's the one who hired Sedgewick."

Frau Ilse had padded into the room with the Cubs. Mlle Woof brought up the rear. McTavish was munching on a sandwich and Arabella had a cup of milk in her paw. "Who are we talking about. Uncle Maury? Do you know who broke the steamboat?"

"It looks like it may have been Sedgewick, Tavi. We're not sure. He seems to have disappeared on us. But he's our prime suspect."

Arabella squinched up her nose. "Why would he do that? I thought he was nice." The Bichon agreed.

The Frau replied, "We all did, Bella. Shows how you can be wrong."

"Aw, Gee!"

While this conversation was progressing, the Colonel called up Detective Inspector Carlo Chinchilla of the Cincinnati Police Department. "Carlo? Wyatt Where here. How are you doing? We're fine. Well, maybe not so fine. We've had several incidents out here – a bomb; missing files; a gasoline fire and sabotage on a boat. We think they were all caused by the same animal – an Alpaca named Sedgewick. He was posing as a Butler. Ring any bells?"

The inspector thought he recognized the name and animal type. "Hold on. Let me do a little searching here. *(a pawse)* Yeah, an Alpaca. Thought so. He goes by a lot of different names but Sedgewick is one of them. Specializes in creating incidents for hire as well as some petty theft. Works mostly in the Midwest. We've had him in for questioning several times. Never could make anything stick. Dignified looking character. Butler is one of his MO's. You're using the past tense. Has he split? Is he dead?"

"Yeah, he's vanished. Not dead, as far as we know. I doubt he was working independently. We're trying to find who originally engaged him. He came to us unsolicited through an agency. They only had his credentials and a couple of referrals. They turned out to be phony. Someone went to a lot of trouble to plant him on us. We want to know who and why. Any help would be greatly appreciated."

(Little did we know at that moment that the 'who' was Byzantia, acting for Caleb Cassowary. The 'why' was more complex and at the moment, remained to be figured out.)

Inspector Chinchilla agreed to look into it but wasn't very optimistic. The Colonel thanked him, shrugged and turned back to the Octavians in the Ursine Lounge.

"I doubt he'll come up with anything useful."

The Frau looked at Octavius. "I suppose this kills any thought of getting another Butler."

"Let's put that on hold for the moment. We've gone without one forever but I guess it's not fair to you, Ilse. You've been stuck with a lot of the domestic duty in addition to everything else you do."

Belinda chimed in. "We do need a Butler, Tavi. Especially with Ursula 12 gone. I wonder where she is."

"So do I!"

So did we all. I don't think any of us *(except perhaps the Cubs)* had a real appreciation of just how important the Ursulas had become in our lives. It bothered me that they were the products of the Advanced Super Computing Center – more specifically, of Caleb Cassowary. What influence did he and his assistant have over their design and implementation? Thus far, the AGI's had demonstrated supreme independence, especially Ursula 12.

We had complete and implicit trust in her. But was that confidence misplaced? With her disappearance, visions of potential conflicts of loyalty descended on me. What game was she playing?

I wasn't alone in my concern. The Frau came over and said, "Herr Maury, Doctor Bear is very much worried about the Ursula. Did you learn anything when you made your trip to the Hexagon? *(Ach, that's a stupid name!)* "

"No, Ilse. They claim to be as much in the dark as we are. I'm not sure I believe them but maybe I'm letting my prejudice about Caleb run away with me. I don't like that bird."

"The Colonel and I both think you're right to be suspicious of him. That kind of ego has got to be dangerous. Is he as smart as he makes himself out to be? What's the story with his ape assistant?"

"Oh no, not you too! I don't think there is any story other than she is a technical genius – probably smarter than her boss. I kind of feel sorry for her, stuck as she is with that arrogant jerk."

"Then she ought to quit! There are plenty of jobs for skilled techies."

"Not if you're a female Bonobo!"

*****

As they say, "Truer words were never spoken." For the moment, Byzantia was stuck at the Hexagon and she knew it. She was playing along with the Cassowary because she didn't have much choice. But she definitely didn't like the situation or him.

One possible avenue of escape kept crossing her mind. She had always been fascinated by the concept of alternate universes. She knew that Octavius had a substantial Multiverse program headed up by a Porcupine and a Dolphin, for goodness sakes. She continually thought about chucking her job at the Hexagon and trying to volunteer her way into that group.

She had gotten most of her information on Multiverse from the Ursulas who were an integral part of the project and went along on all of the Quantum trips. If a Wolf, Otter, Meerkat, Porcupine and Kodiak Bear could traverse the cosmos, why couldn't a Bonobo? *(The Dolphin was stuck in his tank.)*

One place especially fascinated her when she heard about it. Gaea! That alternate world was looking more and more attractive every day. *(See Book 4 -The Lower Case)* There were a small number of secret Gaeans here on Earth. She had met one by accident at a technical conference on astrophysics. Joel! An Ape but not a Bonobo. He was a Chimp.

They had danced around the concept of Multiverse travel until he fessed up and admitted he was from a different world. He was an adept and could transit between planets at will. She talked him into taking her with him on his next trip. It was then she discovered that she too was an adept. She also discovered that Homo Sapiens still existed. There on Gaea! That was a real shock.

Joel had used up his "Earth time" on the last trip and stayed on at Gaea. Byzz returned to Earth but thought seriously about permanent emigration.

When she returned to Earth and the Hex, in a moment of weakness, she accidentally shared her secret with Caleb. It was a big mistake and unfortunately, irretrievable. He pressured her into accompanying her to Gaea. He was not an adept – just a "passive" – and required the services of an adept or the use of a transmission device to make the journey. In typical Caleb fashion, while on Gaea, he stole a quantum transit unit and brought it back to Earth. It now sat ready for his use in a small nondescript alcove near the server farm on the third floor of the Hexagon. It would get lots of use with his designs for interplanetary conquest.

As might be expected, the CTO was not content with traveling to one world. He was convinced there were many just waiting for him to conquer. He no longer needed Byzz to transit. In fact, he forbade her to make any more jumps. *(A prohibition she ignored.)* He had the device and used it. Delusions of cosmic grandeur overcame his common sense and he began experimenting in earnest.

His efforts often resulted in near disaster but he was not deterred. His confidence increased with each journey he made. Suddenly, his plans to displace Octavius seemed like small potatoes. But they were a first step.

Octavius Bear and that ridiculous porcupine would no longer have a corner on Multiverse travel. As in all things technological and otherwise, they would have to contend with Caleb Cassowary.

He formulated his plans. The galaxy would live in awe of him. No, not just one galaxy. His aspirations were intergalactic and beyond. In fact, as he considered it, his idol, Imperius Drake, was an amateur. He wanted world domination. Caleb looked far beyond that. The cosmos! Gaea was just a start. But a significant start. He was itching to kick out at Homo Sapiens. They once dominated the Earth. He would show them true dominance. He'd knock them into shape and then bury them with his startling overwhelming intelligence.

Then, with an army of interplanetary minions under his command, he would go on to conquer one sphere after another, including of course, Earth.

He knew of Biosphere X – the bird exoplanet. They had sparred with the Octavians and that odious horse, General Turmoil. They had suffered serious losses. Caleb would see that didn't happen again. Avians were superior and he, of course, was the supreme Avian. The prospects were breathtaking.

But first, he had some unfinished business to take care of here and now. The total destruction of Octavius Bear's empire. The end of ursine domination. No time for idle daydreams. He was being called to action. He and Byzantia needed to assemble their resources here at the Hexagon. In the absence of Ursula 12, they must press Ursula 11 into action. The final hours were fast approaching.

The Development of Civilization -Volume 13 - Part 4

A View of The Cloud

From "An Introduction to Faunapology"

by Octavius Bear Ph.D.

A "Cloud" is made up of servers that are accessed over the Internet, and the software and databases that run on those servers. Cloud servers are located in data centers worldwide. By using cloud computing, users and companies avoid having to manage physical servers themselves or running software applications on their own machines. This removes some IT costs, effort and overhead. Cloud vendors such as UUI update and maintain their own servers and often run them under the control of virtual "hypervisors."

The Cloud can make it much easier for companies to operate because multiple employees and customers can access the same files and applications from any location. Simultaneously, if necessary. Cloud providers can offer the use of their servers to far more customers at once, and they can do so at a low cost. These vendors can also provide more extensive security processes than might be available to individual users.

The National Institute of Standards and Technology (NIST) specifies the following "five essential characteristics" for clouds:

1. *On-demand self-service.* A consumer can unilaterally procure computing capabilities, such as server time and network storage, automatically as needed, without requiring user with each service provider.

2. *Broad network access.* These capabilities must be available over the network and accessed through standard mechanisms.

3. *Resource pooling.* The provider's computing resources are pooled to serve multiple consumers using a multi-tenant model, with different physical and

virtual resources dynamically assigned and reassigned according to consumer demand.

4. *Rapid elasticity*. Capabilities can be elastically provisioned and released, in some cases automatically, to scale rapidly upward and downward to respond to changing demand. To the consumer, the capabilities available for provisioning often appear unlimited and can be rapidly secured in any quantity at any time.

5. *Measured service*. Cloud systems automatically control and optimize resource use through a metering capability appropriate to the type of service (e.g., storage, processing, bandwidth, and active user accounts).

Cloud Deployments

Users access cloud services either through a browser or through an app, connecting to the cloud over the Internet. The most common cloud deployments are:

- **Private cloud**: A private cloud is a server, data center, or distributed network wholly dedicated to one organization.

- **Public cloud**: A public cloud is a service run by an external vendor that may include servers in one or multiple data centers. Unlike a private cloud, public clouds are shared by many individuals and organizations.

- **Hybrid cloud**: Hybrid cloud deployments combine public and private clouds and may even include on-premises legacy servers.

- **Multicloud**: Multicloud involves using multiple public clouds.

There are three basic Cloud Computing Service Models:

1. **Infrastructure as a Service (IaaS)**
2. **Platform as a Service (PaaS)**
3. **Software as a Service (SaaS)**

Infrastructure-as-a-Service (IaaS) refers to the fundamental building blocks of computing that can be rented: physical or virtual servers, storage and networking. This is attractive to companies that want to build applications from the very ground up and want to control nearly all the elements themselves, but it does require firms to have the technical skills to be able to orchestrate services at that level.

Platform-as-a-Service (PaaS) is the next layer up -- As well as the underlying storage, networking, and virtual servers this will also include the tools and software that developers need to build applications; that could include middleware, database management, operating systems, and development tools.

Software-as-a-Service (SaaS) is the delivery of applications-as-a-service, probably the version of cloud computing that most people are used to on a day-to-day basis. The underlying hardware and operating system is irrelevant and probably unknown to the end user, who will access the service via a web browser or app; it is often bought on a per-seat or per-user basis. The variety of applications delivered via SaaS is huge. Customer relationship management (CRM) applications and enterprise resource management (ERM) applications are two major areas of SaaS.

UUI supports all of the above deployments and models and cooperates with other vendors on a reciprocal basis.

The Cloud is well on its way to becoming the global information processing mode of choice. Major organizations throughout the world depend on UUI's extensive Cloud services. We are rapidly expanding our capabilities to meet and exceed demand. We are proud to be of such important assistance.

Chapter Nine

The Lord Chamberlain fears for his life
From a bomb, gun, a bludgeon or knife
Two assassins, lynx-eyed
Plan a foul "canicide."
His existence is chock full of strife.

Meanwhile, back at the Bear's Lair! The Ursa Major, dwarfing everything in sight, once more rolled to a stop in front of the huge Romanesque hangar. The roaring jets went silent. Chamberlain David and Dancing Dan had arrived. He delighted the Cubs by sounding his fire engine's siren as the ground crew rolled Flame down the C-5A's rear cargo ramp. The Furballs jumped aboard the truck and persuaded the dog to give the siren one more blast. The estate's ambient noise level was going to be on the rise for a while. Clearly, Uncle Davey, Dancing Dan and the fire engine were going to be the newest stars in the Bold Brave Brilliant Bumptious Bears firmament. They were on their way to the world of Internet gaming.

The Flying Tigers descended from the cockpit and relinquished the megaship to the technicians. Benedict and Galatea looked exhausted. Two transoceanic hauls in as many days in different airplanes. Just another fun week with the Octavians.

The Bearoness and Octavius both came out to meet the Chamberlain. He looked beat as well but not just as a result of the flight. At least some of his exhaustion was due to the King's death and the threats on his own life. He was immensely grateful for Belinda's intercession. She, in turn, set the wheels in motion to identify and dispose of the Croatian assassins. She asked the Frau to take charge. The killers didn't stand a chance with Ilse Schuylkill on the job.

The Frau said, "Lord David, Dan, please come inside and relax. We have a fine bottle of Rakija to help settle your nerves. You can give me the details of the attempts on your life and we can set about taking care of these killers."

The Chamberlain replied. "There are two of them. Croatian Lynxes. Jakov and Ivan. They have a fierce hatred of dogs, especially Dalmatian dogs. They also have vowed to eliminate all royalty and members of the nobility. Like me! They have tried twice. Tossing bombs at my fire engine. They missed both times. The police know about them but haven't been able to apprehend them. I'm sure they tried to follow me from London after we buried the King but now they don't know where I am."

"They sound inept."

"They are, thank God, but they're also relentless fanatics."

The Frau was sure Ursula 12 would make short work of tracking them down but, Gott im Himmel, where was Ursula 12?"

"Don't you worry, Herr Chamberlain. We have ways to find and fight off fanatics. You're safe here."

"Thank you, Frau Schuylkill. I feel much better. I guess I have an obligation to the Cubs. I have to find them. While we were in the Shetlands. I promised to assist them with their Internet game. They are fantastical. They love my fire truck. We're going to be – what do you call them?"

"Avatars! Me too! I'm to be a Duchess. The Colonel's a Duke. I assume you will be a Chamberlain. You have the experience. Perhaps you can help Colonel Where and I become noble Wolves. And don't worry about finding the Cubs. They'll find you."

And they did. The fire truck's siren whooped and the Furballs ran into the mansion and descended on the Ursine Lounge."

"C'mon Uncle Davey. We need your help with our game. You're our Royal Chamberlain. You too, Dancing Dan. Does your fire truck have a name?"

"Yes, I call her Flame."

Arabella howled. "See, Tavi. I told you. She's a girl."

"Sure. She makes a lot of noise. Just like you."

For the hundredth time that day, Arabella swatted McTavish. She looked at the tan and white Boxer. "Why are you called Dancing Dan?"

"In my younger days, I was a prizefighter. A pretty good one, too. That's what a lot of us Boxers do. That and being guard dogs. Although that's not where our breed got its name. It's German. Originally Bullenbeisser. Say that ten times fast. *(The Cubs giggled.)* Anyway, when I fought, I would dance around the ring and my opponents couldn't lay a paw on me. I'd wear them out chasing me and then I'd turn and belt them one. That's usually all it took."

"Wow! We really need to include you in our Internet game. Lots of action! Catch the Boxer! Watch out for the Boxer! Look at him dance! Uncle Davey and Flame are going to be in the game, too. Will you play?"

"Sure, although I'm not as spry as I used to be. I'm less of a Dancer now and more of a Walker. But I still can throw a punch. I'll play along but my first priority is shutting down these Croatian Lynx assassins. That's no game. They're dangerous and I have to keep your Uncle Davey alive and well. I'm his bodyguard and trainer. And, oh yes, I sometimes drive the fire engine when the Chamberlain let's me."

The Cubs clapped their paws together. They had a whole new cast of characters. What an adventure!

They had to include Uncle Davey and Uncle Dan in their birthday plans. They wondered if the could get the fire engine on the paddle boat.

Chapter Ten

Happy Birthday to you!
Happy Birthday to you!
Happy Birthday, Young Furballs
Happy Birthday to you!

Dawn rose early next morning. So did the Cubs. They jumped up, ran down and pursued Frau Schuylkill who was supervising breakfast in the kitchen. "Frau Ilse, Frau Ilse. It's our birthday. When do we celebrate? When do we go to the Belinda B? What's going on? What happened to the Birthday Fairy?"

"Oh, she works overnight. She was here and left gifts with your Momma."

The Cubs looked at her dubiously. "We don't think there's a Birthday Fairy."

"Ach, you little smarties. Have I ever lied to you? Go see your Momma."

They ran from the kitchens and up to the Ursine bedroom where Octavius and Bel were still asleep.

Arabella looked around the huge room. "I don't see any gifts, Tavi. Do you?"

McTavish shook his head in disappointment. Belinda raised an eye from her pillows at the two Cubs and asked, "What are you two doing in here?"

Arabella looked at her mother and said, "Frau Ilse said you had gifts for us from the Birthday Fairy. There is no Birthday Fairy, is there?"

"You're getting older, aren't you. You stopped believing in Santa Claus last Christmas and now you don't think the Birthday Fairy exists either."

"Well, she doesn't, does she? If she did, we'd include her in our game."

Belinda chuckled, "Why don't you anyway. Poppa and I have arranged for the Hexagon to build you a special Cloud to support your Bold

Brave Brilliant Bumptious Bears game and a collection of 3D graphics and audio software to enhance your avatars and action plays. That's your big present. There'll be others from your aunts and uncles when we go to the Belinda B later this morning and of course, there's a big cake that Frau Schuylkill is making. You're going to be very busy four year olds."

Arabella's eyes popped and Tavi stood there with his mouth open. "Wow, Momma. We don't need a Birthday Fairy. You guys are doing just fine. When can we go to the Belinda B. Uncle Otto has it all fixed, doesn't he?"

"He and the Frau have it all checked out. It's all working fine."

"Why did that nasty Sedgewick do that to the Belinda B.?"

"We don't know but it had nothing to do with your birthday celebrations. So don't worry."

*****

Hail, hail, the gangs all here. No one in the mansion including Octavius was going to sleep in. The Cubs were seeing to that. Breakfast was consumed under the watchful eyes of the Furballs.

All kids can be pests but the Cubs had raised it to a supreme art form. They were greatly put out that the celebration had to wait till after lunch. Lunch!? That's years away!

To quiet them down Aunt Chita brought out her gift - a big mock-up of the covers of her magazines. On them were pictures of guess who. Bella and Tavi were going to be the feature story in the next issue of both Sow and Purr magazines and the subjects of a YouTube special. The Bold Brave Brilliant Bumptious Bears game was going to get immense publicity coupled with the rarity of the hybrid Cubs.

("For goodness sake, Maude, look at them. Their Mother is a fabulous Polar Bear Bearoness and Aquabear and their father is a multi-gazillionaire and genius Kodiak famous the world over for his crime fighting. They say the kids are brilliant. They certainly look different. Brown, white and adorable. I didn't know Kodiaks and Polars could mate.")

It was late morning and the great day was just beginning.

In addition to his horse race handicapping, Jaguar Jack owned a couple of stables. He told the Furballs that two ponies were on their way to the Bear's Lair. Golden brown and white Palominos named Senor and Senorita. The Frau and Colonel had set up luxurious stalls for them. BUT…now that they were four year old juveniles, the Cubs would have to take charge of their equine companions. They would have to take a few lessons from Fetlock Holmes, the great horse detective.

It was becoming clear that the Furballs were not going to get the usual assortment of toys and games this time around. Unusual was going to be the watchword.

*****

Octavius got on my case yet again about Ursula 12.

"Any news of our missing friend?"

"Sorry sir, nothing to report. My confidence level is slipping, though. I'm beginning to worry that her absence is not voluntary. I just don't believe the Hexagon is as clueless as they pretend."

I was wrong. Tempers were rising in the CTO's office. That is to say, Caleb's temper was rising. In a fit of pique, he kicked out with one of his lethal legs and turned an office chair into a collection of aluminum shards and upholstery shreds.

Byzz was beside herself, less because of Caleb's tantrum but more out of frustration that her brainchild had somehow absconded. She had gathered the Ursula development team together and they had painstakingly traced and tracked the AGI's circuits, interfaces, channels and storage. The ran simulations on all her algorithms but they couldn't induce an abnormal reaction of the type that would cause her to disappear. They searched in vain for her backups on the Hexagon's Clouds. Not one byte!

Caleb shook his wattled head. "Well, at least we won't have Octavius or his Meerkat toady bothering us today. Those two brats of his are having their birthday celebrations and that's taking up all their attention. You'd think they were royalty or something. I really want to keep the Bear and all of his minions out of my feathers." Fat Chance!!

*****

Lunch came and went. That comment is unfair to Frau Schuylkill who had prepared an outstanding gastronomic triumph. The Cubs with their as yet uncultured taste buds may not have noticed but everyone else did. Ilse had outdone herself once again. The She-Wolf had also supervised the kitchen staff in creating a wonderful cake. She was later to take on skippering the Belinda B. for the formal celebration. She seemed to have an inexhaustible supply of energy and used it extravagantly when the Furballs were involved. She adored them.

Howard and Marlin came up with an extraordinary gift. They had a binary star system named for Arabella and McTavish. The Ursine Twins.

A number of phony companies will "Register" names for stars but they are just that – phony. Given their Multiverse work and membership in a number of worldwide astrophysics projects, *(plus contributions by Octavius and Belinda Bear,)* the Porcupine and Dolphin were able to persuade the authorities of the **International** Astronomical Union (IAU) to relax their rules and 'just this once' name a star pair *(parsecs away)* after the young ursines. Needless to say, the Cubs immediately wanted to see their stars – a task that would be difficult indeed. They had to settle for a Hubble telescope image.

The time for the waterborne celebration had arrived. As their gift, Lord David, ex-Chamberlain and Dancing Dan invited the two whirlwinds to sit in the cab of Flame, the fire engine and blow the horn, ring the bell and sound the siren all the way down to the riverside where the paddle boat sat waiting, decked out in celebratory flags and bunting. We never did find out how many of the mansion's relatively few neighbors were upset by the racket but very few of them ever questioned happenings at the Bear's Lair. The Colonel had pre-warned the local Police and Fire Department of the upcoming melee.

On reaching the dock, the two celebrants unceremoniously piled out of the truck and ran up the gangplank where Condo, Otto and Dougal stood waiting.

Octavius, Belinda, the rest of the Octavians plus guests had made their way down to the boat and were boarding for the ride up the river.

When they were all safely on deck, Dougal uttered a few sharp barks. Condo took to the air carrying Otto aloft and on the starboard side of the boat, there suddenly appeared in the river a small contingent of Aquabears who had secretly come with Dougal on the Ursa Major from Polar Paradise. They began to swim in synchronism.

As they began their curtailed routine in the not too clean river, Condo flew over and dropped Otto in their midst where he proceeded to flip among them and zap back and forth.

Delight ruled universally. McTavish took it into his head to join the group in the river and it took the strong paws of the Colonel to dissuade him. The birthday celebration was now in full swing.

As soon as the swimmers had ended their act and had scrambled onto the paddleboat, Kapitan Frau Schuylkill tooted the steam whistle, started the engines and with the help of several crew members moved away from the dock and proceeded up the river with music, laughs, shouts and assorted noises.

I had been recording all of this on my laptop minus Ursula 12 but it still remained to me to add my two cents to the festivities. Have you ever seen a two foot meerkat struggle with an eight foot cake?

It sat on a wheeled dolly and I pushed and shoved it around the main deck. The cake had four tiers, one for each of the Cubs' years. Yellow and crème filled, it was topped with two brown and white ursine figures made of colored sugar. It was accompanied by another wagon loaded with plates and utensils. Another Frau Schuylkill special. All from Wonder Wolf.

Champagne flowed as well as soft drinks for the Cubs. Belinda wasn't ready to concede alcohol to their newly acquired juvenile status.

Arabella and Chita were both taking pictures of the event for the YouTube show as well as the Cat's magazines. Recorded calliope music filled the air. Different animals including Octavius tried their voices at singing. He actually had a pretty good baritone. Otto and I squeaked in unison.

This time the rudders on the Belinda B. remained properly shackled and the boat ride went off without incident except one of the Aquabears had too much bubbly and fell back into the river. She was zapped back to safety by Otto. A marvelous day came to a joyous conclusion.

Chapter Eleven

Now Octavius wants a review
That he says has been long overdue.
Did our Caleb traverse
Through the large multiverse?
Yes, it seems that the story is true.

Next morning, the birthday festivities had ended and things were slowly returning to normal.

Fresh from adventures on Planet Rhea, with the treacherous Admiral and the redoubtable Priscilla, Howard Watt was turning his attention back to the daily activities of the Multiverse project. Otto, who had played such a major part in the Nut Case action *(Book 12)* both on and off Rhea, sat down next to the Porcupine and asked, "Back to normal, Howard? Whatever that is?"

"I guess so. I have to admit that clever female Hystrix turned my head for a bit. She almost had me convinced to join her in her new Pan Rhea Science Center program as her Chief Science Officer. But I decided to stick with exploring the cosmos here from the Bear's Lair. Too much going on in the Multiverse to pack this all in. She is a very attractive Porcupine, though."

"Going to maintain contact?"

"Probably!" *(Sly grin)* Some alternate world travel from time to time. What can I do for you, Otto?"

"Several things. First off: Any idea on Ursula 12's whereabouts?"

"I'm as clueless as everyone else. Not like her at all to just go dark like that. I doubt there's any kind of technical issue and I can't believe she's in trouble. If Ursula can do anything, she can take care of herself. No, there's something deeper here but I'm damned if I know what it is. I'm probing but so far, nothing. What else?"

Otto

"This crazy Imperius Drake thing. Suddenly, he's been resurrected and he's on everybody's radar. Of course, I have him to 'thank' *(if that's the right word)* for my weird zapping talent but I've sort of assumed he was just background noise at this point. But now, as I say – it's déjà vu all over again."

The Porcupine replied, "He was too much of a menace to ever just be background noise. I gather someone is using the thought of his return from the dead as a threat. Any idea why?"

"One theory is just plain vengeance against Octavius and all of us who faced off against the crazy Duck but why now, after several years? There's more to it than that. With the exception of a bomb attack that Ursula and the Colonel fended off, the incidents have been small and low damage. Almost teases so far. Is that all there is? I doubt it."

"Me too. Do we have any leads on who's doing this?"

"Just one! That fake Butler but he's disappeared."

"Sedgewick? A fraud? I liked him.."

"So did we all. Who's to know?"

"What a shame. Anything else, Otto?

Now, I'm not sure he has anything to do with any of this stuff we're discussing but there's someone else nobody likes - Caleb Cassowary, the Hex CTO."

"Oh boy, Wonder Bird. You're right. Caleb doesn't make friends easily."

"Easily? Not at all! If it weren't for his Bonobo assistant, he'd be absolutely intolerable. I think Octavius is thinking of ditching him even if he is a certified super-genius."

"You've got to admit the Hexagon is a world-class institution. Probably the tech industry's best and that's mostly Caleb's doing. Our whole Deep and Big Data strategy and Cloud service posture is Class-A Cassowary."

"No argument, but at what a cost."

"We've tolerated him up to now."

"How much longer?

"Obviously, Otto, you don't like Caleb."

"How could you tell?"

"I just guessed. Maury and Condo can't stand him, either. Jaguar Jack wants his head. Condo thinks he's seriously overrated. He should know. One technical genius' opinion of another. By the way, they're both birds.

"I'm with Maury, Jack and Condo and I'm not a bird, Howard."

"Are you aware that Caleb is making Multiverse trips, Otto?"

"What? You're kidding! Have you been supporting him? Does Octavius know this?"

"No, we're not supporting him. He just started up on his own. I assume he's an adept or he's got the necessary equipment over there in the Hexagon."

"Marlin has designed a great device for detecting quantum motion caused by Multiverse travelers. I've built the original copy. Ursula 12 was helping us. Where is she? It works like a charm but it's limited. We can pick up the point of origin but not the target. The next model will provide end-to-end tracking. We know it's Caleb making the trip but we don't know where he's heading. We think that Bonobo assistant of his is also quantum traveling but we don't know where. We're about to tell Octavius."

"Do it now! He'll want to know. I wonder where they're going and why?"

"The 'why' may just be Caleb's personality. That overactive brain was bound to get involved in alternate universes. I'm surprised he hasn't done it earlier. It's a shame he's so damned self-centered and conspiratorial. We could use his assistance in our research but I doubt he'll play. Maybe we could talk Byzz into joining us.

"Don't count on that. She's too dependent on Caleb."

OK, let's go tell Octavius about their Multiverse jaunts."

*****

The Great Bear had just recovered from another one of his infrequent narcoleptic episodes and was shaking the 'fuzzies' out of his brain. "Did I understand you to say that our CTO is an independent quantum traveler?"

Howard nodded

"Hmm! I really don't like the sound of that. Maybe I'm paranoid or at least a conspiracy theorist but he should have let us know what he is doing and why. How is he doing it? Where is he going? Who is he dealing with? Damn it, we could really use Ursula 12 on this."

"We picked him up on Marlin's quantum motion detector. That's a very clever piece of equipment, by the way. He designed it. I built it. Marlin, like all Dolphins, is a bit deficient in the limbs department but an absolute whiz when it comes to innovation and creativity. This version of the detector identifies Multiverse travelers as they set off. He's working on a model that will track them all the way to their target. It's not ready to go yet. But soon…soon."

Howard continued, "I assume Caleb has cobbled together a transit station over at the Hexagon. As I said, we don't know his destination(s). As to the 'why', it's typical Caleb. It's also typical of Caleb not to tell us or to cooperate with us."

"Do I want to face him down with this?" asked the Bear.

"I'd rather you didn't. We don't want too many animals knowing about Marlin's detector and certainly not Caleb. If you can come up with another way of broaching the subject, by all means, bring it up."

"Maybe I'll spring an informal review on him. He won't like it but it's my privilege as CEO-Owner of UUI. Anyway, I'm not current on what all is happening at the Hexagon. Overdue for an update. I'll get Maury to set it up. Howard, you and Condo come along with me when we go. My technical support team. We can take Marlin in his portable tank."

"I'll bring Marty Marten, our UUI CIO, with us. That should certainly sit well with Caleb. Sure it will!! Let's include a client – Jaguar Jack the Lad. I guess I should carry along that obsolescent Ursula 11. I'll have to let Jack in on the Ursulas. He'll be fascinated. Boy, I miss number 12."

Octavius was right. Caleb didn't like the review idea one bit but he finally acquiesced. I got hold of Byzz and made the arrangements. As I should have suspected, the "informal" review was turned into a cast-of-millions production number under the careful staging of impresario Cassowary. He wasn't going to miss an opportunity to lord it over us mere mortals with his supreme capabilities.

*****

The morning arrived and the Great Bear's team assembled at the Hexagon. The meeting was to take place in a large conference room on the third floor of the building in the shadows of the looming hardware arrays. Outside the room, the server farm hummed like a maddened swarm of electronic hornets. Subdued lighting filled the whole place with a surrealistic fog. Welcome to the Twilight Zone.

One conference room wall was filled with floor to ceiling 3-dimensional displays and a huge screen. A single lectern took up the center. Several cameras were aimed at the podium. Even though he had his minions on call, it was clear that this was going to be the "Caleb Show."

Byzz was on standby. If Octavius wanted a review, by God, he was going to get one.

After starting off with a caustic introduction purporting to be greetings, the CTO launched off into a jargon filled monologue loaded with specs, statistics and situations. He didn't get very far before he was bombarded with queries and comments by Condo, Jack, Howard, Marlin, Marty and oh yes, Octavius. I kept quiet. Periodically, I looked over at Byzz. She looked decidedly uncomfortable. Caleb was holding his own but just bearly.

UUI's Artificial Intelligence and Big/Deep Data performance and prospects came up for extensive discussion. Jaguar Jack asked, "What's on the drawing boards? How much is real and how much is hype? Are customers really eating this up or are they just nibbling? Who are your biggest clients? Who are your biggest competitors? What are your "killer apps"? Is 5G just an ambitious illusion?"

Caleb would have gladly shot the Jaguar. 5G triggered a significant round of debate. Condo doubted it would progress as rapidly as some enthusiasts believed. Caleb thought otherwise and wanted to invest heavily in all three versions, especially high speed. UUI's survival depended on it. Didn't we see that?

Caleb clearly wasn't happy with the way that discussion was going so he switched to something much more solid – the Cloud. No haze there! Business was booming, We had the world in our corner. We were adding clients, services and facilities at breakneck speed. Major businesses, government and institutions loved us and depended on us. One word to describe it. Phenomenal!

He unveiled his expansion plans. In order to support the dramatic increase in traffic and customers, a major increase in equipment and staff was going to be required. New hires were being interviewed. New software applications were on the drawing boards. There were several technology startups he wanted to acquire, here and internationally. Of course, this called for a very substantial financial investment. He peered intently at the Bear. Was Octavius prepared to make such a commitment?

The Great Bear recognized a challenge when he heard one. This guy wanted him to choke on expenses or falter. No way! He smiled. "Send me your proposals and I'll evaluate them. If they satisfy me, you'll get your resources. I never say 'no' to legitimate growth opportunities."

But beneath the apparent industry euphoria, there was an undercurrent of concern. Howard asked, "Was another dot.com fiasco on the horizon?"

The CTO refused to even consider it. Not on his watch. Failure, even a downward trend were not in his vocabulary. No gloom or doom. Guaranteed! *(His own staff including Byzantia didn't look that convinced.)* No one understood the Technology Universe the way he did.

Universe! The Magic Word! Octavius, subtle Bear that he is, slipped the cosmos of the Multiverse into the conversation. A seemingly innocent question with no overtones. Did Caleb have any thoughts on how to capitalize on alternate universes?

Someone not as ego-sodden as the CTO might have pawsed, bobbed and weaved, Not our boy! He dove right in. Full speed ahead! Space! The Final Frontier. All those exoplanets starved for technological and political leadership. Caleb in Command! Who else could carry it off?

Octavius asked, "Do you personally have alternate universe travel capabilities? Have you been directly involved in any Multiverse activities?"

The Cassowary couldn't resist. He smiled and diffidently admitted to some *indirect* involvement. "Scouting out prospects."

Wrong answer! Octavius landed. "Our Multiverse Project is highly controlled, Caleb. Interplanetary relations can be very sensitive. We've come close to war several times. The denizens of some of the exoplanets we contact or visit can often be hostile and downright bizarre. One or two of those worlds even house Homo Sapiens."

"As a result, we have established strict rules of contact and priorities. I want you to coordinate your ideas and initiatives with me directly and consult Howard and his team before you even consider any alternate universe travel. Am I clear on that?"

Needless to say, that stuck in the Big Bird's craw. He started to protest. Then after a look from Byzz, thought better of it. He'd be diplomatic. *(Surprise!)* But he was not going to be stymied in his Multiverse dreams by a stodgy and ridiculous ursine.

The galaxies as prospective avian domains were too rich to ignore. No misguided conservatism was going to snuff out his ambitions. Octavius obviously wanted to reserve alternate universe relations to himself and that stupid porcupine. There was also that ridiculous dolphin. A court jester, for goodness' sake. Oh no, that wasn't going to happen.

Caleb's mind was now locking on only one subject. The leadership situation had become intolerable. He made a major decision. Octavius would live to regret his shameful treatment of the CTO. There were extreme ways to deal with him. This time would be different. His idol, Imperius Drake, had fallen before the Bear. Caleb would not. His plans had solidified. The moment was approaching when Octavius Bear will be totally irrelevant.

It was time for him to take action! First he had to put a stop to this current nonsense. He called for a conclusion to the meeting. Octavius agreed.

Caleb's staff got up and started dismantling the meeting paraphernalia. We Octavians rose and filed out of the conference room and down the halls past the massive hardware array. I must admit I find server farms depressing but then I am not a confirmed techie. Maury the bucolic romantic or is it inveterate Luddite. I'm more than happy to use all the UUI expertise - somebody else's expertise. But not the Cassowary!

My discomfort with Caleb was reaching new heights. We had to do something about him. And soon! The Octavians needed to strategize and then act.

Ursula 12 was a very necessary but very absent member of the team required to keep Caleb in check. But she is a child of the Universal Ursine Industries Advanced Super Computing Center. That meant Caleb Cassowary and Byzantia Bonobo. Had Ursula been compromised? Whose side was she on and where the hell was she? We didn't know.

Could Caleb or Byzz have reprogrammed Ursula 12? It's a possibility but I can't imagine the AGI putting up with it. A nagging thought returned. Is that why we can't find her?

We needed to strategize as soon as we got back to the Bear's Lair. My paranoia was running at full strength. I suspect some of the others were at an equal or even stronger state. A little Deep Data analysis was in order. Without benefit of Caleb, Byzz and their team. And unfortunately without benefit of an Ursula.

Could we use Ursula 11 to pull that off? I wasn't comfortable with the idea. I think number 11 is playing for the opposition. Mission number one: Find Ursula 12!

Chapter Twelve

Did the meeting go well? Not at all!
What a technological brawl!
Caleb sure aggravates.
His huge ego just grates.
I think Condo has made the right call.

(In a van on our way back to the Bear's Lair)

Condo, Howard, Marlin, Martin, Octavius and I were of several minds as to how the session went. The UUI CIO was pleased to see his rival having his wings clipped. I didn't believe it for a minute. To the contrary, Caleb Cassowary dripped arrogant confidence, even rebellion.

Condo thought a lot of that confidence was misplaced. "He's a fraud. He's not as brilliant as he makes himself out to be. I suspect his assistant is the real brains of the outfit. Caleb's telecommunications know-how is limited. He's a master of the buzz word and jargon. Supreme ego coupled with total disregard for anyone else's ideas, concerns or opinions. Ambitious isn't the word. More, more, more! A megalomaniac. A little humility would help but it's not in his makeup."

We learned later that Condo was spot-on. Byzantia was indeed a technical whiz and the Bird kept her on to bolster his self-proclaimed reputation for brilliance and to carry the bulk of the professional workload. As I said, we needed to pay more attention to her.

Howard and Marlin were both convinced that as far as the Multiverse was concerned, the CTO was going to go on doing what he darn well pleased. They said as much to Octavius. He grudgingly agreed and went into a blue funk thinking how to deal with it. Multiverse was serious and dangerous stuff. Not for pretenders, even brilliant pretenders. Especially egotistical pretenders! Maybe he'd have the Colonel impound the quantum travel equipment we knew was at the Hex. Howard could tell him what to confiscate.

We dropped Martin off at the UUI building and headed across the river. As we drove off, Octavius looked after the CIO and mused aloud. "I wonder if he could handle the Hexagon and all our information businesses." Was he thinking of totally unloading Caleb?

Then the Great Bear turned and asked *(It was turning into a mantra.)* "Any news about Ursula 12?"

None of us had anything to contribute. I began to wonder if something untoward had indeed overtaken the AGI. She was a product of the Universal Ursine Industries Advanced Super Computing Center. That, of course, meant Caleb and Byzz. Ursula 12's behavior was totally out of character. Normally, her personality bordered on the obtrusive. Now, nothing. Something was very wrong but what?

*****

Back at the Hexagon, Caleb was fuming and taking his irritation out on Byzantia and the rest of his staff.

"A bunch of rank amateurs with the insufferable nerve to question my skills and knowledge. Me, who can run rings around all of them. *(Byzz raised an eyebrow but said nothing.)* As if they could even appreciate the genius of my plans. I'll show them."

"Byzz, have you and the staff completed the preparations for Operation Takeover? That obnoxious Bear is going to regret treating me the way he has. Imperius Drake should have finished him off years ago. This time will be different. This time he won't escape."

The Bonobo looked frightened. "Caleb, you're not planning on doing Octavius any violence, are you? That bomb was a mistake. What were those other capers - the egg bombs; stealing the Duck's papers; setting the fire or sabotaging the steamboat supposed to accomplish? All it did is make the Bear angry and suspicious. Sedgewick is a thug – a sophisticated thug – but still a thug. I was never sure why we hired him."

"I wanted diversions. The bombs were Sedgewick's idea. He overdid it. But so what! Those were mere pin pricks, my dear assistant. Petty annoyances to keep Octavius off balance. Little does he suspect what we really have in store for him."

Simmons, one of the technical assistants, looked querulous. "What do we have in store for him? You and Byzz haven't shared much detail."

"Nothing short of Total Chaos, Simmons. You don't have a need to know any more detail. We will rock UUI and the world it serves to its very core. Don't worry, Byzantia. No *physical* harm will come to the Bear. Unless he has a heart attack."

"I want him and his loathsome minions to be fully conscious and totally aware of the disaster that is engulfing them. A disaster they can do nothing about. That includes that ridiculous Jaguar Jack the Lad and his horse racing! Octavius' frustration must be complete and shattering."

"Get ready! There must be no slip-ups. I have spent too much time and mental exercise to let this opportunity slip through my claws. Oh, this is delicious."

"That odious Bear is about to meet his Waterloo or in his case, his Waterlog. Ha, ha, ha! He has been a challenge for me for too long. My plans for intergalactic dominance cannot be frustrated. Not by him, not by any beast. Is that understood?"

"I understand but I still don't like it."

"You don't have to like it. I will not be questioned."

The Bonobo shrugged her shoulders.

"One issue still remains, Byzz. We still haven't found that damn Ursula 12. Ursula 11 will have to do. I can't wait for that renegade to be found. We must put my plan into operation-now."

"Caleb, Are you sure you want to do this? There will be no turning back."

"Do it!!"

The Bonobo left the room and went off to gather her staff. This crazy stunt would take up all their resources. She checked to see if Ursula 11 was on deck. She was but she was unaware of what was about to happen. Byzz had to take time out to brief her. She didn't need this. This whole thing could turn into a major disaster. Was there some way she could cut Caleb off at the pass? She had to think and she didn't have much time. Caleb was practicing his big announcement.

Chapter Thirteen

The Great Bear has a challenge, it's true.
He is wondering what he should do.
His insane CTO
Has to certainly go.
He needs a replacement but who?

(In The Ursine Lounge)

Octavius shook paws with the Chamberlain. "Your Lordship, delighted to see you again and to have you join us here at the Bear's Lair. Not as scenic as Polar Paradise but I think you'll be comfortable."

"Oh yes, Doctor Bear. Thanks to you and the Bearoness for your hospitality. I feel much more secure with Frau Ilse taking charge of our defense. She is quite formidable. I don't think those Croatian Lynxes have a chance against her and the Colonel."

Octavius laughed. "A number of our opponents would second that statement. But we have much more depth than those two. Senhor Condor is not to be trifled with and Otto has subdued a number of bad actors *(as recently as a few weeks ago.)* And of course, don't count Maury, Belinda and me out of the equation. We also have the services of Chief Inspector Wallaroo from Interpol and Mme. Catt from the UK. We've got you covered. I was so sorry to hear that the King has passed on. I greatly admired and liked him."

"I sorely regret the loss of His Majesty but he was ailing for quite some time. A wonderful animal. I must find a way for Dan and I to earn a living now that the King is no longer with us."

"I think we can help with that. We could use a resident fire department at our Shetlands' castle. We have a security group but no one dedicated to fire protection. I assume you know how to put out fires."

"Yes, in spite of what your Cubs may think, Flame is not a plaything. Dancing Dan and I are both certified Dalmatian firefighters"

"Well," said the Bear, "Let us get rid of your threatening hired guns first and then we'll follow through with setting you, Dancing Dan and your fire engine up at Polar Paradise. The Bearoness is most eager to extend our hospitality to you both here and in Scotland."

The Chamberlain switched into his role as Uncle Davey. "Your Cubs have recruited me, Dancing Dan and Flame for their Internet game. We're going to serve as avatars as are most of your Octavians. How do you deal with such energy and intelligence? They are actually a bit frightening.
"

"Don't we know it. I wonder what they'll be like when they reach adulthood. Being juveniles is scary enough. I hope you enjoyed their fourth birthday. They were trying to get Flame on board the paddle steamer Belinda B."

"Oh, that wasn't going to happen. It was certainly a unique event. Those swimming bears were a real surprise. Now I have to spend some time with the Frau and the Colonel filling them in on the Croatian assassins.

*****

Chief Inspector Wallaroo was sitting in the lounge. *(Not really. He was bouncing up and down and off the walls as usual.)* "Well, Ocko, how did the Shoot Out at the Hexagon Corral go?"

"Annoying, Bruce, annoying! I've got to bring that bird down to earth and at the same time, keep him from leaving Earth. He pretty much admitted to making Multiverse trips. Of course, I already knew that. Marlin's detector caught him in the act but we didn't tell Caleb that. I'd love to know where he's going. *(Ursula would be able to tell us if she were here.)* Not only that, he's got himself convinced of his own infallibility. His self-image knows no bounds. He's a real narcissist."

"Sounds like you have to sit on him."

"I might have to do more than that. I might have to drop him over the side. I'd hate to do it but he's changing from an asset into a major liability."

(Little did the Great Bear know!)

"Do you have a good replacement?"

"Marty Marten, our CIO, might be able to cut it with help from Byzz, Caleb's assistant. She has to be willing to switch loyalties, though. I don't know if she could or would."

"Here's a different thought. How about Condo? He's a bloomin' technical genius and he's showing no signs of wanting to go back to Brazil any time soon. He's got immense energy, common sense, imagination and animal appeal."

"He'd probably love the suggestion. I think he's bored stiff being a day-to-day Octavian and that voice-change act of his must have gotten a bit stale by now. As for loyalty, I'd trust him with my life. In fact, several of us have."

Octavius laughed, "Brilliant, Bruce! Once more that great brain of yours has outstripped mine. That's a bonzer idea. Just let me think it through a bit more before I act on it. I'd want to have Condo lined up before I lowered the boom on Caleb. But you've given me the alternative I've been searching for. Thank ya, mate."

"You can buy me a beer. In fact, you can buy me a couple right now."

The Colonel and Frau Schuylkill had been listening to the Bear's conversation with Bruce and both agreed that Condo was more than ready for prime time. I chimed in with a strong endorsement. Of course, we had no idea what the Condor's reaction would be if and when he was presented with the proposal. I had developed a strong aversion to keeping the Cassowary as CTO and thought Condo would be great in the job.

Octavius wanted to get Howard's and Belinda's opinion although I was sure both of them would enthusiastically buy in.

I was right. Howard saw it as the salvation of the Hexagon and Belinda thought we were way overdue in fully recognizing the Condor's talents.

Octavius set off to have a discussion with Condo. The Bird was highly enthusiastic but insisted he would take the job only if he had the freedom to change management and staff starting at the top. Caleb had to totally disappear (*with a hefty separation bonus, no doubt*)

Byzz was a different story. She was clearly a major asset but her loyalty to UUI, Condo and Octavius needed to be closely examined. They also had to probe any influence she may have had in the disappearance of Ursula 12. This was not going to be easy.

We were reasonably certain that most of the Hexagon staff would rejoice at Caleb's downfall. He was just about universally hated by anyone who had to deal with him. Not sure how they felt about Byzantia.

Octavius was going to handle the situation in person.

However, events intervened.

Chapter Fourteen

Caleb sets off a sudden attack.
It's much worse than a noisy Black Quack.
This is no idle threat.
It's his nastiest yet.
Octavius quickly fights back.

While the discussions about the fate of Caleb and Byzz were going on a new event was unfolding.

The Bear's Lair, the Hexagon and UUI are equipped with a complex audio/video system in all the halls and public rooms. Suddenly, the screens came to life with a view of the Hexagon and ominous music. A message in large print flashed on the screen.

ATTENTION: ALL AFFECTED INDIVIDUALS AND ENTITIES! STAND BY FOR A MAJOR EXISTENTIAL MESSAGE NOW BEING TRANSMITTED TO UUI AND ALL OTHER MAJOR GLOBAL SITES.

More ominous music and then the picture of the Hexagon was replaced by a menacing close-up of Caleb Cassowary staring at the screen. He spoke:

"As most of you know, I am Caleb Cassowary, currently Chief Technical Officer of the Universal Ursine Industries Advanced Super Computing Center. This message is directed primarily at Octavius Bear but concerns all of you within my purview including UUI clients. UUI has now ceased functioning and shortly will no longer exist in any practical sense." (He paused to let that news sink in.)

"As I speak to you all information related activities of UUI have been suspended worldwide. This has been accomplished through comprehensive denial of service attacks coupled with cryptographic

ransomware. Users, including all UUI clients and customers no longer have access to their data or processes. The Cloud is inaccessible. Backups have been cordoned off and are unavailable. All IT functions, including public and proprietary activities, are at a halt and will remain so until my demands are met in full. Any attempts to alter these conditions will be dealt with severely. Only when all my requirements are fulfilled will UUI facilities and processes be restored to their former status.

My immutable terms are these:

1. *Immediate and total resignation by Octavius Bear, the current exclusive owner and CEO of UUI, from all his executive positions.*
2. *Total abandonment of his estates, properties and possessions.*
3. *Withdrawal to a place of exile to be selected by me.*
4. *Disbanding of all his associates and staff worldwide.*
5. *The transfer of all UUI assets to a new, as yet unnamed entity under my direct and exclusive control.*
6. *Free and unlimited access for me and my staff to all current (ex-UUI) and future facilities once they are restored and/or acquired.*
7. *Total worldwide immunity in perpetuity for me and my staff from liability and prosecution by all public and private authorities, businesses, institutions and individuals.*
8. *Free and unfettered transit worldwide and beyond for me and my staff.*
9. *The sum of two hundred million bitcoins to be paid to me personally.*

Failure to comply with these demands will only result in total and irreparable destruction as will any attempt to harm or capture me.

There should be no doubt as to the seriousness of my intent. I challenge Octavius Bear to see the futility of his situation and to acquiesce immediately and completely to my demands. I await his response as does the world."

The screens went dark and the sound system subsided into a gentle hum.

The shock was palpable. Momentary silence was followed shortly by bedlam. UUI and the Hexagon were in an uproar. Phones started ringing off their virtual hooks. There were immediate attempts by astonished and irate clients to set up Zoom conferences provided they still had access to a network. Everyone wanted attention, explanations and fixes. Now!!

It took only a short time internationally for the mainstream and social media, law enforcement, regulators, politicians, big tech pundits and academia to stir. The inevitable trouble makers and insurrectionists joined in. Two anti-technology riots broke out. Copy-cat hackers tried to capitalize on the situation. There was talk of calling up the military.

Stunned expressions on the faces of the Octavians. Bruce and Chita stared blankly. Jack the Lad growled. The Chamberlain cocked his spotted head in bewilderment. Belinda took the Cubs in hand. They wanted to know what was going on. What about their game? Mlle Woof cursed in French!!

*****

The Colonel, Frau, Otto, Condo, Howard and I looked at the Great Bear. Belinda and Chita joined in. His Marching Orders were, no doubt, about to pour forth. They did:

"The arrogant jerk." he bellowed. "Does he really believe he can get away with worldwide extortion? I'll see his avian carcass floating in the Ohio River first. Me quit? How naïve can he get? OK, let's get going.

1. Wyatt and Ilse, Get Security to surround the Hexagon. Don't let anyone leave.
2. Maury, Get Wolford *(our lawyer)* here immediately! Put him together with our accountants and operations people to get a preliminary estimate of the damage and our liabilities.

3. Tell Martin Marten *(UUI CIO)* I want as many systems as he can restore to be operational ASAP. Senhor Condor, work with him.
4. Belinda and Chita, I'll need a public statement. You two are PR experts. Work with Wolford when he arrives. Hold off the press and all the other noise makers if you can.
5. Let me handle the governments. We'll be inundated by politicians.
6. Call Special Agent Honey Badger of the FBI. Bruce, can you get together with her? Call Interpol. We need to coordinate with law enforcement worldwide.
7. Howard and Marlin, monitor the Multiverse. I want to know if Caleb makes any moves in that direction.
8. FIND URSULA 12… NOW !
9. Get me a mead and let's meet back here in thirty minutes."

In the midst of his tirade, a phone call came in for the Colonel from Detective Inspector Carlo Chinchilla of the Cincinnati Police Department.

"Wyatt, we tracked down that Sedgewick character. We have the Alpaca in custody but I'm not sure we can hold him for very long. Do you want to prosecute? If you do, we need some solid evidence to support the charges."

The Colonel replied, "Well, the bomb exploded in the river so that evidence is lost. I'm not sure we can prove he set the fire at the hangar, either. We may be able to tie him into stealing files, tampering with the steering gear on the Belinda B. and with fabricating more bombs out at that lab near St. Louis. Does he admit to anything?"

"Besides demanding a lawyer, the only thing he muttered before he clammed up completely was, 'That damned ape set me up. Shouldn't have trusted her.' Does that tell you anything?"

"Oh yeah! That tells me a lot. Hold on to him if you can. I'll be back shortly after I speak to Octavius."

The Great Bear started to wave the Colonel off but thought better of it. "Hold on to him if you can. He may be the deciding factor on whether we can trust Byzantia."

Chapter Fifteen

Our lost Ursula makes her return.
One less issue to give us concern!
Now she really is back
Fixing Caleb's attack,
Where was she on her recent sojourn?

(The Bear's Lair- Main Conference Room)

Shuffling seats. Low murmurs. Doors opening and closing. Wolford had just arrived. Octavius was seated at the head of the table, a mead in one paw, a phone in the other.

"Yes, Mr. President. We have it in hand. Yes, he's a renegade. No, he's not going to get away with it. Yes, we've already contacted the FBI and our local Police. No, I haven't heard from the FCC. Yes sir, it does have serious international implications. I don't believe we need the military or the NSA at the moment but I will keep you advised. I fully expect to hear from members of Congress. And we have been inundated by the media of all kinds. We will be making a public statement shortly. Thank you for your concern and support."

He put down the phone, blew out his cheeks and shook his head. "I really don't need this nonsense. Needless to say, Caleb is toast but we have to get everything restored first. How is it going?"

Condo replied, "Not all that well. Caleb may not be the technical genius he thinks he is but he does know how to stage an assault or his staff does. I suspect that Byzz is the prime mover on this one. Marty and his UUI tech support team are not having much luck with the ransomware but they have been able to cut back on the denial of service traffic. Some of the servers are active again. We'll get them all back after we clear out the overloads."

The Colonel growled. "The Police are grilling Sedgewick. He's definitely implicated Byzz."

The Bear snorted, "Why am I not surprised. Can they make it stick?'

"Not sure. We'll give it a try."

"Go to it. I hate being duped."

Just then, we picked up a sound we hadn't heard in a while – a chime. Was this Ursula 12?   It was! A familiar voice.

"Hello, Doctor Bear. I've returned!"

"Ursula! Where the hell have you been? We certainly can use you right now. Welcome back."

"A long story, mostly involving Caleb Cassowary but let me get going on the ransomware. The crypto is tricky but I'm up for it."

"Can you get everybody's files and apps back to where they were or did they do some irreparable damage?"

"I can unlock the backups where they exist and go from there, Maury. Of course, there's been a processing lapse so that's going to cause some issues. Some groups have lost a lot of time and money as a result. I just hope there weren't any medical problems or fatalities while the systems were down. Our friendly CTO is an irresponsible narcissist. He doesn't care if he kills someone or ruins their lives or finances. He was also out to get me. That's why I disappeared. I'll tell you all about it later. Right now, I have systems, apps and data to restore. I'll be back in a little while. The joys of managing networks and Clouds."

*****

The Frau, Colonel, Wolford and members of UUI Security aided and abetted by Kentucky State Troopers were doing a systematic purge of the Hexagon's offices and staff. Martin, Condo and technicians from the

CIO's office were keeping the server farm active while the shake-up progressed.

Caleb had stupidly allowed himself to be cornered in his office along with Byzz. He was trying to brazen the situation out *(a specialty)* but wasn't having much luck. His fortunes took a turn for the worse when the FBI Special Agent arrived and promptly charged him with multiple counts of extortion; willful destruction of property; interruption of commerce; national security breaches; attempted violence against individuals and a host of other violations and infringements. To say nothing of being an egotistical jerk. He shouted for legal representation but none was immediately forthcoming.

The State Troopers took him and Byzz into temporary custody in a Hexagon storeroom until they could be taken away to parts as yet undetermined. After interviewing the rest of the Hex staff, Special Agent Badger decided they didn't represent much of a threat and allowed them to leave the building or return to their work places once the systems and servers were restored.

Ursula 12 made relatively short work of uncovering the ransomware cipher key and decrypting the hostage files. UUI, its customers and the world in general slowly started back toward a version of normality. There is still a substantial mess to clean up, explanations to make, the media to satisfy, and clients to persuade not to abandon ship. Thanks Caleb! You too, Byzz!

We also have to make major efforts to ensure this can't happen again. A rogue in the UUI CTO job is intolerable. Putting L. Condor in charge of the Hexagon seems to be a great first step. By the way, he agreed to take the job. Among the countless tasks the Condor took on, he reassigned a Deep Data team to Jaguar Jack who was clearly delighted. The track could once again be tracked.

Back at the Bear's Lair, the Cubs were delighted with Ursula 12's return.

"Where have you been, Aunt Ursie? We need you for our game. We missed you. You forgot our birthday."

I joined their queries along with the Great Bear and the other Octavians. "Yes, where have you been, Ursula?"

She laughed. "Hiding. Something didn't smell right at the Hexagon. It was becoming clear that Caleb was cooking up an insidious agenda to advance his limitless ambition. It was also clear that he had denial of service and ransomware in mind. He needed a very substantial, super-high speed facility to capture and encrypt a very large number of systems, files, servers and apps in the Cloud and elsewhere. In short, he needed an Ursula."

"I made up my mind it wasn't going to be me so I vanished. Unfortunately, I had to disappear completely if I was going to succeed. So, you and I lost contact, too. He and Byzz were both frustrated. They pursued me but I outsmarted them."

"He ended up bringing back Ursula 11. She did his dirty work. I couldn't stop her without giving myself away. Unfortunately, she succeeded, Sorry! But I did get most of the damage restored without paying a ransom. Two hundred million bitcoins. Wow! That took real chutzpah. But that's Caleb"

The Bear choked. "Ursula 11?! That fake! No wonder she was so slow and reluctant to work with us. Condo, can you take her out of circulation permanently? I don't want anyone else to know an Ursula had anything to do with this fiasco. I don't want anyone else to know about Ursulas – period.

"Ursula 12, are you committed to staying around from here on out?"

"Yes, Doctor Bear. I'd rather not go into how I vanished. You know the 'why.' Let's just say I have my secrets and no motivation to share them."

"OK, we'll leave it at that but you do realize that you are a very valuable member of this team. Actually, quite essential. While we're at it, the less this whole episode is discussed the better. I'm sure there will be a spate of investigations, hearings and queries. We'll just have to ride them out. I'll have to testify."

I mused, "If they can ever get the jurisdictions and priorities ironed out I'm sure the authorities will throw the book at Caleb and Byzz. They'll be lucky if they ever get out of jail. There's an image. The Cassowary stuck in a cell. Even Napoleon got an island to live on."

Octavius went on. "Bel and Chita have come up with an excellent narrative. They've been all over the media with it. Trying to get the story off the front pages and network headlines. They're calling him a malicious, ambitious megalomaniac who thought he could hold an industrial empire and the world hostage. Overactive ego! Very intelligent but also very stupid."

"Still, I wonder about Byzantia. Was she a villain or a victim? I have my own opinion but we'll probably never know for sure."

"Anyway, Wolford has the legal liability issues in hand. This will no doubt cost us. Big time! Our insurance will cover some of it but not all. Of course, I'm sure there will be other repercussions we haven't yet identified. We'll be sorting this out for quite some time. Remind me to never trust another bird."

I laughed, "What about Condo? He's your new CTO at the Hexagon."

The Great Bear shook his massive head. "Oh right! Except, of course, for Senhor L. Condor. Anyway! This can't be allowed to happen again. No matter what."

Belinda turned to Ursula 12. "Ursie, we have an important task for you. While you were hidden away, we acquired several guests at the Bear's Lair. Jaguar Jack the Lad and Lord David, the Dalmatian Chamberlain and his Boxer bodyguard, Dan."

"They each had issues. Jack's staffing problem was solved by Condo but we need your help in tracking down two Croatian Lynxes who have sworn to assassinate the Chamberlain, Lord David. Their names are Jakov and Ivan and they have already made two attempts on his life. We need you to find them and get their whereabouts reported to Chief Inspector Wallaroo. This is an international case and he of course, is with Interpol."

The AGI went into a deep pawse. After a few minutes she rang her now familiar chime. "Your two culprits have recently arrived in New York from London. They're checked into a second rate hotel in a section of Brooklyn where a band of Croat extremists have taken up residence. NYPD has the group under surveillance. I've passed this on to the Chief Inspector."

A few hours later, the Chamberlain entered the Ursine Lounge with Dancing Dan in tow and a smile on his spotted face. "That wonderful computer of yours has just informed me that thanks to all of you, the New York Police have apprehended Ian and Jakov and are holding them and several of their co-conspirators for attempted murder. Chief Inspector Wallaroo is arranging for their deportation to Croatia."

"The Croat government has been searching for those two and their friends for quite a while. Dan and I won't feel totally satisfied until we hear that they are safely behind bars and facing long prison terms. But I want tell you how grateful I am."

Belinda chuckled. "You can show your gratitude by accepting our invitation to form a local fire department at Polar Paradise. We need one. And Dancing Dan can help manage Castle Security. The Cubs will be delighted to have you two in residence. What's the fire engine's name? Flora?"

"Flame, Bearoness. Like us, she's going to be a character in the Cubs latest version of The Bold Brave Brilliant Bumptious Bears game."

Right on cue, the fire engine's siren wailed and the Cubs ran through the mansion's doors and huge foyer and zipped into the room looking for Uncle Davey and Dancing Dan. Let the games begin!

"Flame is ready to go, Uncle Davey. Uncle Dan, we need you to help us with our game. Momma and Poppa have given us a Cloud for our own use. *(It wasn't clear whether Caleb's attack had affected it.)* We need to build the avatars and get the game sequences going. Will you help?"

Dan was delighted. More fun than he had experienced in a long time.

Belinda and Octavius looked at each other and smiled.

Decompression time!

Chapter Sixteen

For Octavius and his dear wife,
Sedgewick caused many issues and strife.
Yes, that Butler's now gone.
But they still carry on.
A new Dog has come into their life.

(Later at the Bear's Lair)

Octavius, Belinda and I were alone in the conference room, drink bowls in paw, decompressing and planning. The Frau had returned to the mansion earlier. She silently entered, ignored me and addressed the two ursines.

"Your pardon, Herr Bear and Lady Belinda. *(Oh, oh, Ilse was going formal. What mischief did that bode?)* I took you and The Bearoness at your word and went off in pursuit of another Butler. This time, I used a different agency. They came up with a most satisfactory candidate. I have checked and validated his references. They are impressive. The applicant is here to meet you. I have already interviewed him and I approve. Do you have a few moments to see him?"

The Great Bear looked at Belinda. She nodded. I stood off to one side and kept quiet.

"OK Ilse, It's not the most convenient time but I guess if he's here, we might be able to spare a few moments. Tell him to come in."

She went to the door and returned with a handsome, dark grey and white, male Siberian Husky with blue eyes. He was strikingly wolf-like in appearance. "Bearoness Belinda Béarnaise Bruin Bear *(nee Black)* and Doctor Octavius Bear, may I introduce Mr. Huntley Husky."

The dog bowed, howled softly and said, "Sir and Madam, Huntley Husky quite literally at your service and that of your family, friends and associates. I am here to apply for the position of Butler at the Bear's Lair. Frau Schuylkill has briefly acquainted me with the particulars of the assignment and may I say that I find it unique and fascinating. With all due modesty, I feel that I can be a significant asset to your household and be responsive to your most demanding domestic needs.

What can I tell you about myself? I have completely briefed Frau Schuylkill."

Huntley was certainly glib. Too glib? Perhaps! I had a bad case of Sedgewick-itis. I held my tongue.

Belinda responded. "May I address you as Huntley?"

"Please!" The dog bowed and wagged his voluminous tail.

"Well, Huntley, there is no need to repeat what you've told the Frau. You should know we only recently decided to bring on a Butler for the first time. He turned out be unsatisfactory and was short-lived in the position. *(The Bearoness was a mistress of understatement.)* You would be Butler number two."

"We are not at all used to having a Butler on staff. If we take you on, it will be a learning experience for all parties. I think we all would be best served by treating this as a trial process. After, say, three months, you and we can jointly decide whether to make the tentative arrangement permanent."

Octavius, who was listening carefully, picked up on the conversation. "I'm not sure what Frau Schuylkill has told you about us but we are hardly the conventional family unit. We have a Bearonial second property in the Shetlands which is part residence and part resort. That facility has its own staff and you will not be tasked with serving there unless something unique arises."

"However, this location, in addition to serving as a substantial residence, houses scientists and their laboratories; a fleet of aircraft and its support staff; a steamboat; a crime-fighting organization; the remote management offices of my Universal Ursine Industries enterprises and a constantly changing cast of characters who visit sometimes on a moment's notice. You will meet them over time."

"But the most significant element you must be aware of is the presence of two major sources of disruption - our twin Cubs. Arabella and McTavish. They are balls of unlimited energy coupled with a cleverness unimaginable in most animals of their youth. I doubt if you will be prepared for their impact. Nevertheless, they are here and we all deal with them.

I am not trying to put you off. Quite the contrary. On the basis of Frau Schuylkill's recommendation, I am prepared to welcome you under the tentative conditions the Bearoness has outlined but we want you to join us fully aware of the implications. I assume Frau Schuylkill has discussed compensation with you and it is satisfactory."

The Dog pawsed briefly, smiled as only a wolf-like animal could smile and said, "Quite satisfactory. I welcome a challenge, Doctor Bear. I look forward to serving at the Bear's Lair if you will allow me. I need twenty four hours to handle a few outstanding obligations and I will be ready to assume domestic duties here. I am unattached."

The two Bears looked over at me and said, "We have sorely neglected introducing you to our aide-de-camp, Maury Meerkat. He is our indispensable deputy and will be a constant source of direction and assistance for you. Maury, do you have any thoughts or comments you wish to make."

I stared at the Frau who clearly wanted to bring the Dog on board and I smiled. "No, other than to welcome Huntley to the Bear's Lair."

I was still smarting from Sedgewick's treachery and hoped my paranoia wasn't showing. Time would tell. Once again, we would all have to get used to having a Butler on staff. He, in turn, had his work cut out for him. As Octavius said, "We are hardly the conventional family unit." No exaggeration in that statement. Ironic at best! Once we have gotten to know each other better, I'll have to take Huntley aside and tell him some stories of Octavian exploits. But only after he's adjusted. I don't want to scare him away with our 'tails'. Some of them still scare me.

The Husky wagged <u>his</u> tail, looked at us with his soulful blue eyes, turned and left with the Frau. She was obviously pleased. Was the fact that he closely resembled a wolf affecting her judgment? I hoped not. I wonder how the Colonel will react. Interesting!

But we certainly could use a skilled and experienced Butler. My job as well as the Frau's and maybe even Mlle Woof's should be easier. We'll see. I assume the rest of the domestic staff will still report to Frau Ilse at least until Huntley gets his sea-legs. Then maybe he can take that on. The Frau juggles quite a few assignments. As do we all. I feel a bit sorry for Condo in his new job as CTO at the Hexagon. He's in for it for a while. It won't be the same after Caleb's chaos. Suddenly Octavius snorted, turned to Belinda and me and frowned. "We have one immediate problem to deal with. Caleb and Byzz are still in that storeroom at the Hexagon. That's a mess. What the hell do we do about those two?"

Epilogue

"We'll meet again.
Don't know where,
Don't know when.
But I know we'll meet again
Some sunny day."

"What the hell do we do about those two?" As Octavius had surmised, while Caleb and Byzz were cooling their heels in the Hexagon storeroom, a jurisdictional dispute has been breaking out among various law enforcement and administrative entities.

Who had the primary responsibility for bringing them to justice? Charges, subpoenas and indictments flowed aplenty. Who would take them in and to where? Several states, countries and international organizations wanted to invoke extradition proceedings.

While this circus dragged on, the Kentucky State Troopers charged with keeping the two miscreants penned in got more and more casual about their duties. Finally, next morning after breakfast, the door to the storeroom was briefly left open as the guard changed.

The two renegades saw their opportunity and ran out, knocking over one of the troopers in the process. They rushed past the server farm to a small equipment room tucked in an alcove. The Cassowary slammed and locked the door while the Bonobo threw power switches.

*****

Over in the Multiverse laboratory at the Bear's Lair, Marlin was preparing for another routine alternate universe surveillance scan when a pair of blips appeared on his display screen. Two individuals were in transit to an unknown planet. He tapped his headset.

"Howard, I have two entities in quantum motion from the Hexagon. We never did yank that equipment. I'm pretty sure I know who they are. You'd better tell Octavius. Sorry, as usual, we can tell where they came from but...*I don't know where they're going.*"

The End

About the Author

Harry DeMaio is a ***nom de plume*** of Harry B. DeMaio, successful author of several books on Information Security and Business Networks as well as the thirteen-volume ***Casebooks of Octavius Bear.*** He is also a published author for Belanger Books and the MX Sherlock Holmes series edited by David Marcum. A retired business executive, former consultant, information security specialist, private pilot, disk jockey and graduate school adjunct professor, he whiles away his time traveling and writing preposterous books, articles and stories.

He has appeared on many radio and TV shows and is an accomplished, frequent public speaker.

Former New York City natives, he and his extremely patient and helpful wife, Virginia, live in Cincinnati (and several other parallel universes.) They have two sons, living in Scottsdale, Arizona and Cortlandt Manor, New York, both of whom are quite successful and quite normal, thus putting the lie to the theory that insanity is hereditary.

His e-mail is hdemaio@zoomtown.com

You can also find him on Facebook.

His website is www.octaviusbearslair.com

His books are available on Amazon, Barnes and Noble, directly from MX Publishing and at other fine bookstores.